THE MAD

AFRICAN
LANGUAGE
LITERATURES
in Translation

THE MAD

Ignatius T. Mabasa

Translated by J. Tsitsi Mutiti

THE UNIVERSITY OF GEORGIA PRESS

ATHENS

Publication of this book was made possible, in part, by a generous gift from Karen and Art Dunning.

Published in North America in 2026
by the University of Georgia Press
Athens, Georgia 30602
www.ugapress.org

Designed by Erin Kirk
Set in Minion Pro
Printed and bound by Sheridan Books, Inc.

The paper in this book meets the guidelines for permanence and durability of the Committee on Production Guidelines for Book Longevity of the Council on Library Resources.

Printed in the United States of America
30 29 28 27 26 P 5 4 3 2 1

EU Authorized Representative
Easy Access System Europe—Mustamäe tee 50, 10621 Tallinn, Estonia,
gpsr.requests@easproject.com

Library of Congress Cataloging-in-Publication Data

Names: Mabasa, Ignatius Tirivangani, 1971– author | Mutiti, J. Tsitsi translator
Title: The mad / Ignatius T. Mabasa ; translated by J. Tsitsi Mutiti.
Other titles: Mapenzi. English | African language literatures in translation
Description: Athens : The University of Georgia Press, 2026. | Series: African language literatures in translation
Identifiers: LCCN 2025047061 | ISBN 9780820376943 hardback | ISBN 9780820376936 paperback | ISBN 9780820376950 epub | ISBN 9780820376967 pdf
Classification: LCC PL8681.9.M13 M3713 2026 | DDC 896.3975—dc23
LC record available at https://lccn.loc.gov/2025047061

First published in the Shona language
by College Press
Harare, Zimbabwe.

First published in English in 2025 in the United Kingdom
by amaBooks and Carnelian Heart Publishing

Translator's Note

I've been asked many times, Why translation and why *Mapenzi*? The simple answer is that I fell in love with Hamundigone's personality, which Memory Chirere describes as uncensored and sometimes utterly warm and likeable. I loved Bunny's and Magi's introspection. I loved all the characters because they are so relatable. These are not people to be pitied but strong people living the best they can, people making the most of whatever resources are available to them.

The second reason is that I wanted to improve my halting Shona literacy. I could read Shona but not comfortably, because I only had a few years of formal Shona education. What better way to improve on my Shona language than by reading books in Shona? When I finished the reading *Mapenzi* for the first time, it stayed in my head. I think we need a word for books that stay with you for a long time, the way we have the word "earworm" in reference to songs that when heard continue playing in our head. While this book earworm was playing in my head, I started wondering how Hamundigone would sound in English. Or Mai Jazz, how would her degree in popotology sound in English? Years ago, while at University of Zimbabwe, I met Nhamo Mhiripiri, and he introduced me to Russian literature. I became an enthusiastic fan of Gogol, Dostoevsky, Pushkin, Tolstoy, and others. Every week would find me haunting the library in search of my next Russian novel. At some point, Nhamo and I had a conversation about the beauty of translation and how all these great books would have remained inaccessible to most of the world if they had remained in Russian. I asked, Why haven't our great novels like Charles Mungoshi's *Kunyarara hakusi kutaura?*

been translated into English? and he responded, You could translate your favorite books. I laughed and forgot about it, because I thought he was teasing me—but here we are. The seed planted so long ago germinated when I started asking myself, Could I really do it? Could I really translate a book in Shona into English and produce something reasonably resembling the original? And just like that I decided to try. This translation basically started its life as a private exercise aimed at improving my Shona and as an attempt to see if I could do it—and here we are so many years later. The exercise has borne fruit.

What a journey it had been, a learning experience all the way. The very first paragraph in the first line "*ndinoparadza zvisina mutsindo sehwai*," which I translated as "I am a lethal and silent destroyer, like ram." When I first read *hwai* I was thinking of sheep. The word "sheep" is not normally associated with anything menacing. I had a conversation with colleagues who set me right by explaining how dangerous the male of the species can be—hence the choice of ram in the translation.

The other thing I learned is how much we take our mother language for granted. Its words are so deeply embedded in our minds that we usually don't really think about the concepts these words represent. When translating, analysis becomes necessary so that a fitting word or phrase can be found. Sometimes this is a simple process; other times it's a wrestling match.

Language is a patchwork made with words, culture, and other beliefs peculiar to the speakers of language. Patchwork was my grandmother Gogo's favorite pastime. She was one of those people who could never be idle, and patchwork was what she did when there was no work for her to do. She was able to do so much patchwork because my mother's side hustle of sewing and selling clothes produced a lot of fabric scraps for Gogo's work. It was my job to sort through the scraps left over from sewing and pack all the suitable pieces into "Box raGogo." Gogo made her patchwork into pillows, quilts, and sometimes tote bags for us, her grandchildren. Sometimes one of her grandchildren would say, "I want a quilt just like the one you made for Mukoma Hope." She would try, but it was not always possible to replicate Mukoma Hope's quilt, because the contents of Box raGogo depended on what my mother was sewing at the time. I would dig into Box raGogo under her instructions looking for the bits she wanted. Sometimes we'd find fabrics in the right colors but with the wrong textures. Or the right fabric but the wrong colors. Ultimately, the second quilt would be its own thing but with a greater or lesser resemblance to Mukoma Hope's quilt depending on the time that had passed.

In some ways translation is very much like Gogo trying to use scraps from box B to replicate a quilt made with scraps from box A. Take a simple concept like walking. Box A will have words like *famba*, *fora*, *kanyaira*, *pesvaira*, *bhidhaira*, *dhanaira*, *digaira*, *chakwaira*, maybe even *pesu-pesu* or *tutya-tutya*. Box B will have walk, march, stroll, tread, waddle, toddle, prance, sashay, power walk, and so on. Sometimes the correspondence is immediately obvious, but other times the choice from box B takes a bit of thought and improvising. Sometimes box B might not have a corresponding word at all, and one has to make do with a phrase or even a sentence. Take the word *Munhu*. That's simple enough to translate into English. But what if we *chimunhu*? Or *Zimunhu*? Or a concept like *ngozi*, which is intrinsic to Shona beliefs. Would "karma" be good enough to convey the idea? "Avenging spirit"? Or does it need a paragraph to convey the full meaning of what ngozi is?

This means that the final product bears some resemblance (hopefully a lot) but is in a way its own thing. Ultimately, translation is an approximation, and as a translator one has to accept that some things will be lost in translation; nuances, some emotional content, cultural aspects. The idea is to minimize these losses as much as possible—and also to avoid new things creeping into the story because of cultural differences or differences in beliefs and values between the original audience the book was written for and the target audience of the translation.

Language and culture are so closely intertwined that any work in a particular language is also a reflection of that culture: a culture likely to be foreign to the targeted reader. This presents a problem of how to handle these cultural differences. I think writers of science fiction and fantasy who create worlds that have their peculiar cultures and rules also experience the same problems of how to convey these worlds to their readers in a way that the readers will understand. Writers like Frank Herbert in is Dune series or Isaac Asimov in his Foundation series do this by using quotations from various documents and commentaries said to exist in those worlds. The quotations bring the readers to the author by explaining and educating the readers about the world they enter when they read these books. Likewise the translators can do a similar thing through footnotes and glossaries. Other authors like Anne Leckie in her Ancillary series and Ursula Le Guin in her Earthsea series simply get on with their story, assuming the reader will be able to infer what kind of world it is and how things work in that world from the story. There is little detouring to explain the culture and values of these worlds. This is similar to how translators can bring the author to the reader in the same way. This second approach puts greater emphasis on entertaining the reader, while the first approach looks to educate the reader. *The Mad* underwent a transition from the first approach to the second approach at the suggestion of the editors. I think they made a good call. As I say, this has been a learning experience for me. My original purpose in doing this translation for myself was superseded by a new purpose to translate for an actual audience.

Finally, our cultures determine our values, and this is an area where a translator has to make decisions about whether to take the values of the target audience into consideration. I did not do this but translated everything as is because sexist attitudes, homophobia, and violence are intrinsic to who we are. Happily, the editors remembered to put this disclaimer at the beginning of the book concerning these issues.

I'd like to thank Ignatius Mabasa for trusting me with the work of translating his creation, and I hope I have not mutilated it too badly. I would like to thank Anne Morris and Samantha Vhazure, editors, for the superb work they did in polishing my rough work. And thanks to amaBooks and Carnelian Heart Publishing for believing in this translation enough to publish it.

—J. TSITSI MUTITI

THE MAD

A Human

You know me; I don't waste time and I don't mince my words. You know that I am a lethal and silent destroyer, like a ram, and have no fear of my shadow. However, the horns in my mind are entwining into a knot. The bark string tying them together is hard to undo. This string is not from the bark of a mupfuti or a munhondo tree. Rather, it is a strange thing with eyes and teeth. My mind is now numbed by a new disease in Zimbabwe, which is neither AIDS nor any kind of STD. You look at what you are and realize something needs changing but find no time, strength, hope, or even the place to begin. Have you ever heard that harsh words will wreck your heart? There are some people who die lamenting, their hearts long rotted away, or else they find what they long for only when they have no further interest in it, after they have washed their hands like Pilate. And, if they do find it, they will not know what to do with it. As for me, I no longer seek much; here on earth we are akin to those warming themselves at the evening fire, called away one by one to supper, only to meet again in dreams.

Time. Let us learn to give time a chance. What is the hurry after all? What is it you are rushing for? A grasshopper in a man's palm does not know the size of the man. A tree in a forest does not know that it has a hollow in which a squirrel lives with her family. A millipede crawling along a tarred road does not know that the road was built by humans for their vehicles. I don't know when the echoes within me shall be silenced. The chameleon eyes keep probing and delving. Will I ever feel refreshed, breathing clear mountain air? The water in which we wash our bodies and souls is murky and our lives sordid.

In the times in which we are living, I would not be surprised if a mutamba tree bore pumpkins. Is it any wonder we are afraid of other people? These days I fear nothing but fear itself and that terrifies me. Death only makes me laugh now. I seek it and it flees! But when we meet, we shall defy each other. Let me just get this bit of bark to clear away the debris piling up in my mind so that I can speak to you without rocks and all sorts of bits in my mouth. I see footprints. I hear footsteps. Do you not see them? Do you not hear them? Am I awake or asleep? Is this really you or your shadow? If it is really you, then poverty fits you well, like a well-tailored jacket.

Teacher

An oldish man was eating boiled maize and drinking beer. He bit into the maize and chewed as if chewing on a piece of bark to make string. His temples bobbed in rhythm with his jaws, as do two pestles in the same mortar being wielded alternately by two women. After chewing for a while, he took a sip of his beer and swallowed. His eyes were small and sunken, and he appeared very alert because they never remained long in one place; he was akin to the sentinel baboon that watches to ensure that its fellows are not caught in the act of stealing from the fields. He wore a moderately smart suit, in a lovely shade, though it was slightly soiled. You needed to look at it closely though to realize that it needed dry-cleaning.

With the beer bottle on the floor between his feet, he read *The Sunday Mail*, tracking the words with his index finger and smiling to himself. People glanced at him and walked on by. He took a pen out of his pocket and underlined some words, then gently nodded his head. After checking his watch, he got up abruptly as if suffering from a sudden attack of diarrhea. He snatched up his beer bottle and made his way to the station for kombis to Harare. On arriving there he saluted and stood to attention like a policeman or a soldier. He said to a woman with a baby strapped to her back, "Eee . . . Mai Kambeu . . . Is it Kambeu or

Kamunhikwi? I forget, I have taught so many kids. Never mind, mother of Kagaka. But do you know I was once a teacher?"

He was silent for a while, watching the kombis arriving and departing, then he resumed, "What the hell are all you people doing? Oh my, just what are you doing? How do you expect these vehicles to move? Take cover, you'll be hit by the enemy bullets. Hey! I said what are you doing? Hmm, I'd better keep quiet, else they'll say I'm mad." He lifted the bottle to his lips and gulped, eyes squeezed tightly as if drinking bitter medicine. He sighed "Aahh" as he took the bottle away from his lips. He looked toward the kombis again. "Uh uh, they just don't stop, do they? Stubborn, exactly like a beard. Shave it today and tomorrow it's sprouting again until you get tired of that shaving game."

"What are they doing, baba?" the woman with her baby strapped to her back asked, perplexed by the old man's behavior.

"A-aa, Mai Kampira, don't you see it? Look and see. They are leaping all over the place and then diving into the kombis, both the stationary ones and the moving ones. Then they suddenly stop! I'm just surprised; aren't they scared of dying? Did you see the red kombi with tires like Maud's cheeks that is going to Harare? Never mind. Did you say something?"

There was a brief silence before he remarked, "Hoo ya-a, I was once a teacher, actually. A real teacher, writing on the board with chalk and teaching your kids, but they fired me. They say I am crazy. Would you accept that—me mad, amai? Do I look as if I might be raving, do you think? Someone who taught kids this past year and even had some getting fifteen points to go to varsity. Do you know what fifteen points mean, amai? Very hard to achieve; it takes a dedicated pupil and an expert teacher. Nuts! I don't know who can diagnose this kind of crazy. Me, crazy? Now that's really nuts. No one likes a profound thinker who speaks his mind. That's me, wide awake and always on the ball. I'm a genius but they call me mad. Do they even recognize madness when they see it? Amai, do you know madness? Of the sort in which people have to be kept bound in heavy chains? People make jokes out of madness, honestly. By God, they are all nuts." He paused, adjusting his trousers and watching the people at the kombis. He turned to look at the woman with a baby strapped to her back as if he expected her to say something.

The woman simply tittered, eyes downcast as if he were flirting with her. She said nothing.

"Oh, so everyone thinks I'm mad, do they? You are laughing at me, aren't you, Mai Kampira? Why do you laugh at me? I bet you are nuts as well. Apart from myself, only one teacher in the whole school, Mr. Shamuyarira, realizes that I am perfectly sane. I showed my students how to critique literature; to think deeply, analyze and sift through the concepts. I taught them to see the grains of sugar at the bottom of a cup full of tea, to sort out the rocks from ruins and rebuild them into a mighty fortress in the mind. This needs a free mind, a fearless mind, flowing intrepidly like the white waters of the mighty Zambezi over Victoria Falls. Who does it fear, for what? It simply flows quietly without coughing or quaking. Foaming ideas and thoughts should never be repressed. A mind bubbling with ideas is what is needed. That's all!"

The man looked up at the sky and started declaiming, gesturing with the maize cob.

"Hear me, hear me, I say!
Hear me, the voice of a mad one,
A voice hated as a debt is hated.
You may look away, but still you hear me,
I'll vex you like a vagabond's avenging spirit.
Go your way saying it is madness
But it will cook you slowly like trotters
And leave you pulpy like paper in the rain.

Hear that voice, hear it,
It will be like a hook stuck
In the mouth of the one fish
That got away,
Constant reminder of its brush
With a fisherman.

Hear me, oh hear!
Feel me like a punch in the eye!
Hear me, the mighty voice that wakes a baby,
Me, the voice you would wish silent like the rocks.
The voice you would wish cold like a corpse.
The voice that speaks what you
would rather not hear.

I'm not a lion drawn on a page in a book,
Whose mouth you may let the children touch.
I'm not a deserted house in a ghost town
Home to lizards and rats, oh no!
The militant within me is an avenging spirit
That causes one to be a shabby vagabond.
His words kill and eat your sleep at night,
He is a small, loose stone in your shoe
Nibbling at your sole with each step,
Yet you cannot stop to remove it
Because your sock has gaping holes.
He is like dregs left behind in your gums
Burdening your tongue which continually probes
The caves inside your cheeks.
He wrecks the head like a spade shoveling manure.

He eats up your ideas as the mechanic's greasy overalls
  consume soap,
Beware, he will hit you where you cannot rub with your hand,
Where you can't show your mother that you've been beaten.
That voice is a subtle but frightening little flame,
Later on, burning forests.
So listen well, like a woman of fellowship receiving the gospel.

Is this decent, I ask you, is it pleasing?
Answer me this tricky riddle then:
The pot was burnt cooking sadza on the fire
But only the plates from the shelf
Went to grace the table?"

He became silent, then strolled to a large muhacha tree and proceeded to irrigate it with urine. Some people merely laughed, but others, bemused, shook their heads and asked what he was talking about. He came back, zip gaping carelessly, and boarded a kombi that was calling for passengers to Harare.

Wars

"These evening kombis are a problem," he said, settling himself by the window.

"Yeah, you're right, my friend. The touts have been calling for passengers for a while now, and yet the kombi is still only half full," agreed a man who seemed to be tired of waiting. He had not noticed it was the teacher speaking.

"Yeah, of course I'm right, mate," the teacher responded, sipping from his bottle, which was wrapped in an oily paper bag. Bits of the maize he had been eating stuck to his mouth and beard.

"Oh boy, I do enjoy Bindura but, hey kombi conductor, let's go, Harare awaits us," the teacher called to the conductor, who was hanging around outside waiting for passengers to fill the minibus.

"Good, if it's waiting for you, you won't find it gone then, will you?" the conductor answered.

"Ah conductor, you should have been a lawyer, you are so good with words. Ha, young man, you're too sharp. If I were a teacher I would surely give you a star, young man. Here, take this fifty-dollar note." He handed the money to the conductor and his fellow passengers looked at him, their faces questioning why they had ever got into a kombi with such a nut. They could not understand why a person could just give away money so casually, hard as it was to get. That was just too much.

"Thanks, old chap," the conductor replied, slipping the note into the pocket of his white, blue-stitched shirt.

"Ah! Isn't this young man slow? Is there anything for free these days? Thanks you say, do you think I just gave that to you? That's my fare to Harare. I'm giving it to you now in case I fall asleep on the way. I do not like to be woken up, so there's your money now." The people's laughter annoyed the conductor.

"Old man, you shouldn't be so crafty," the conductor exclaimed, making out a ticket.

"Conductor, is tobacco allowed in here?" the teacher asked. There arose a commotion of muttering from fellow passengers, although no one would clearly state their case.

"Eh, good people, forgive me. I've not yet killed anyone, so don't whinge. Do you even know what sort of tobacco I'm talking about?" the teacher asked, looking around at all the grumbling faces.

They all looked stonily at him and didn't bother to reply.

"All I want is to take my snuff." His fellow commuters laughed with relief, thinking how unlike most madmen he was. It wasn't clear if he was even mad—he could just be drunk.

"So why did you ask the conductor if tobacco is allowed when you knew you were not going to smoke?" a dark-faced man asked.

"Ah, I was worried about sneezing and splattering everybody. Ha ha ha ha ha! You can't get me and that's the truth. That was my war name, Hamundigone—you can't get the better of me, and it's still true," the teacher replied, laughing uproariously. A young woman sitting next to him, her hair done in long braids, sneered contemptuously to show her exasperation with the old man.

"Aha, finally, the kombi is leaving, now let me sleep. If I nap, then I will be alert when I get to Harare. Don't let me miss my stop, young lady, OK?" he commented, glancing at the fuming young woman. She did not answer but looked away, frowning even more.

"Ah young lady, do you think I am flirting with you? If anyone ever told you that you are beautiful, they lied. I have seen girls more beautiful than you who are well mannered, slim, who, even when they are angry, are stunningly beautiful as if they had a flower in full bloom between their lips. And ah, when they smile, you could jump up and dance. Let me tell you, they are as lovely as payday. Not like you. When you frown your face looks like a pile of dry dung. Why would a face look so ugly as if dishing out smelly stuff? Did you buy artificial hair so that you would look like a decent person? You probably had to buy it because yours looks like the scorched strings of a primus stove. Why frown at me? What have I done to you? I'm simply enjoying myself. I'm not cursing you or anything like that. It is people like you who can't live in peace with others that we used to kill during the war. If you want to stay in your own world, why not go into the mountains and live there? On second thought, don't go to the mountains because you will disturb the peace of the baboons. Don't make my BP rise on such a lovely evening, do you hear? Why do you frown at me when no one frowned at you when you got on the kombi? Why sneer at me—what have I done? If you did not want to speak to me, you should just have kept quiet rather than diss me like that. I am human just like you and I have the right to be where I want to be and to speak my mind freely. This is no longer Smith's time; that's why we fought the war. I am not stinking, am I? I took a bath this morning using sweet-scented Lifebouy soap. Can't you smell it on me? I brushed my teeth with Colgate. See, I even have a tube in my jacket pocket." He pulled his jacket open and brought out a tube of Colgate and a toothbrush from an overburdened inner pocket.

"Young lady, if you are not careful, you'll turn into a witch. In fact, I made a mistake; it seems you're one already. Take me to the police if you like and report that I have labeled you a witch. I fear fokol, nothing but fear itself. Let me take a nap and stop talking, but please don't strangle me while I sleep. I don't want to die yet. The enemy bullets failed to kill me, so I must live a bit longer. I still have to overcome many problems before I die—if it is at all possible.

"Eee vanamai, please forgive me if I have overreacted. All you women are my mothers, truly, for you looked after us so well when we were fighting in the bush with the boys. If anyone is really wise, and I mean genuinely wise, instead of those who lie, faking knowledge, they should give medals of honor to all the brave mothers out there. I myself have no authority to bestow any awards on you mothers, but you are my heroes. The mothers really helped us win the war. They actually fought the war together with us. That's why I don't want to offend you mothers. If I speak badly, just tell me and I will be silent. It's just that I wanted to correct my little sister here, whom you mothers as teachers have failed to educate about not frowning at others. Pamberi nekunzwisisa—forward with understanding, young lady! Down with hooligans, thugs, and the unruly who piss in the common well!"

No one responded.

The teacher laughed, not from amusement, but rather from pique, then examined the faces of his fellow passengers. They looked uncomfortable. He laughed again, "Yeah, you people are now so out of touch that you can't answer our slogan? Anyway, it's not your fault. I know the people at fault and it's those who have so pissed on you that even a war slogan has become nauseating. Never fear, their insults will come to an end, as Chimbetu sang. Let's go Chimbetu."

The teacher bowed his head and there was silence in the minibus. People were sitting silently as though at a wake. No one dared say a thing. They seemed afraid, or perhaps they had other things on their minds. Whatever, who can know what is contained in the domes perched above our necks?

It was getting dark outside. The minibus was now speeding on the approach to Glendale. Many people had fallen asleep after the teacher went quiet. No one dared so much as cough, since the teacher looked furious and no one knew what he would say or do next.

The teacher suddenly roused himself in the silence, snapped his head up like a cobra, and, with shining eyes, glanced from side to side, looking at his fellow passengers. "Sleep simply won't come to me. If it was not for this sellout who annoyed me, I might have fallen asleep. Good people in here, I'm boxed in. I feel overcooked and so you should try not to add more firewood."

"Your sister here was truly in the wrong," a woman seated behind the driver responded placatingly.

"If only people would not do that to me. Please get me right, I'm not saying I'm God, but sometimes I feel like an overfull bag that won't close. Why are people egotistical like ZUPCO, which thought it would always remain top dog? Why should some people want to pester others? So smug like a razor blade, which, unlike a knife, has more than one cutting edge. Look now, my beer is finished, I can't sleep, and I can't read my Mungoshi since there are no lights in this minibus. So what do I do? You guys are blessed, you don't see any bloody daggers before your eyes, you have no problems that steal your sleep and you can easily drift off even during travel on a bumpy road. What about me? Hmm?"

He looked at the girl's face gleaming with perspiration. There was a fierce silence, broken only by the purring of the engine.

"I don't sleep much unless I drink. I hear war songs warring in my head. What really goes on there? As you see me, I have been through much and much has been through me. Zimbabwe has mauled me so that even today the wounds remain unhealed and septic like the scars that I brought back from Mozambique after the war. Zimbabwe has scooped out my spirit, the same way you do when digging a grave. It has left a gaping hole that can't be closed. I have seen much in life for which I have no words to explain."

He brought out his handkerchief in the duskiness of the car's interior and wiped off his perspiration. "No, don't think that I am mad. When I'm out of my mind I will let you know. Right now I am still myself. Let me tell you the truth. They fired me from my job like a dog. I told myself that it doesn't matter because sometimes the goat is accused of having eaten the meat while the dogs stand nearby licking their muzzles. So I decided to go to Bindura to sort out my pension so that I could go to my rural home—kumusha. I was no longer interested in their wrangles. I'm still not interested. Where can you find the strength to argue with someone and convince them that you aren't crazy? It's not possible. That only makes them think your madness has stepped up a notch. So I did not say goodbye to the headteacher. He's actually one of those fools who regard others as if they were mad enough to need tying up in plough chains. I only told Shamuyarira, the only teacher who seemed to appreciate me. I told him that I was leaving and left some of my property in his care. I did not say goodbye to my students, who were my friends and who understood me very well and knew I was most definitely not mad. So I got onto the bus to Bindura—as you know Bindura is not far from Mavhuradonha. I went straight to the ministry offices. They all knew my story and so did not ask me much as they could already see a mad man before their eyes. I did not stay long in Bindura as I was told to go to Ambassador House in Harare, the ministry head office. I told them that I had no money to go to Harare. I was actually waiting for payday the following week. They gave me money then and there. It was just a plan to get me out of their faces so that I would not contaminate them. I got into a kombi, same as I did today, and was soon in Harare. At the entrance on the ground floor a security guard accosted me and said, 'Sir, I am afraid you are late, can you come back tomorrow for assistance?'

"How can you say that without hearing what the person's problem is? Good people, some things are truly amazing. It was only just past three, still within working hours, but the ministry guys had already finished work.

"I left the place quietly and went to check if there was any money in my bank account. I only had ten dollars left in my pocket, just enough to get me to my sister's. I planned to sleep at my sister Maud's in Zengeza, who would probably give me the bus fare back home if things didn't work out.

"I only went to the ATM to try my luck, but it was as good as trying to catch a fish in a dish I knew was empty. I didn't expect to find any money in that account. I was lucky that I found just over $200 in there. I'm not sure where it came from as I had cleared everything in the account. Perhaps our great spirits, Nehanda and Chaminuka, seeing that I was being wronged, gave me the money. Do you suppose Nehanda and Chaminuka know about ATMs? They don't know about technology, so it couldn't have been them. It was God who gave it to me, since He knows everything. Even the Nehandas are in awe of him. I guess the money must be from the little interest that the banks throw our way from time to time after making profits from our savings. But I never expected to find over twenty dollars, so God had smiled on me. Does God ever smile, I wonder? He must, since he created people and they smile. And we are made in his image, are we not? But I think some people are not much of an image of God considering their treatment of others. They stamp on others with hard hooves."

He sat silently for a while, softly clapping his hands in surrender and grimacing in the dark.

"Anyway, I withdrew the whole lot and went back to the Ambassador Hotel on Union Avenue to have one or two beers. It was better for me to withdraw it all since I would be going back kumusha where there are no banks. Even then, I knew I was not crazy as they had alleged when they dismissed me. And if any of you think I'm mad, you are the mad ones. Fools!

"You know what? The guys who worked at the ministry whose offices were closed were at the Ambassador Hotel. I found them there, drinking. I could tell from their conversation that they worked in the Ministry of Education. It made me furious, but I stopped myself telling them off in case they thought me mad. So I drank my beer quietly among those folk who leave their jackets in their offices to do their work. In truth, they leave bottles of Coca-Cola half drunk so that anyone stumbling into their empty office will see the bottle and think that the officer is just somewhere nearby. Meanwhile, the officer will be in Marondera or even as far as Bhora. People!

"I got so drunk that I fell asleep sitting on the stool. While I slept, pickpockets pilfered the little money I had left, together with the wallet. I was only awoken by the cleaners the following morning soon after dawn. Now I truly appreciate Dambudzo Marechera's sufferings as he carried around his idiosyncratic ideas, with those who didn't think the same way as him calling him insane. If you saw a lunatic staring you in the face, would you know one?

"After being thrown out of the bar by the cleaners, I stood outside patting my pockets for some change, only to find them empty. How can anyone be so shameless as to pinch someone's wallet and not even return their metal ID? As if he could become me. Or maybe he wanted to use the sheet metal to make a tin can? I feel certain some people are quite mad. I mean, why steal something you don't even need? Perhaps it is demonic.

"All I had left were the clothes on my back. I saw that some people were already rushing to work, you know those who start work at the crack of dawn. The trouble with certain people is that they only ask whether there's a job without bothering to ask what the working hours will be. So they get jobs where the time they have to start is the time that some, like us teachers, will only just be getting out of bed to get ready for work. Oh, by the way, I'm no longer a teacher. I keep forgetting that. Just imagine sparing crazy, incompetent folk like Mrs. Mapuranga, who drifts off during her lessons. Whereas I teach with passion. I could climb on top of the table to demonstrate this, yet I'm the one who gets kicked in the butt. Well, it's all good.

"So, I passed Union Avenue and headed toward the parliament building, then swung round to Africa Unity Square. I wanted to wash my face before figuring out what to do next. My head was throbbing as if, inside it, people danced mercilessly to a thudding drum. You mothers are blessed you don't drink. Do you know having a hangover is like being really sick? On my way into the park I met some vendors slicing and buttering bread for sale. This roused sharp hunger pangs in my belly. My last meal had been the previous morning. The handful of mopani worms Shamuyarira's wife gave me hardly counted as a meal; better to say I had not eaten all of the previous day. I had eaten nothing with my drinks the night before. Even though some say drink is food, it still cannot compare with sadza. We forget to eat before we drink, silly isn't it?"

No one replied. All were listening avidly for what happened next in the teacher's yarn.

"I stood by the bread cart, pretending to think, then I asked, 'How much is a slice, boys?'

" 'Two dollars.'

"The vendor didn't even bother to look at me as he spread jam that looked like blood clots on the bread. I paused for a bit, and then said to myself, 'Let me ask him for some bread, maybe he'll take pity on me.' Hunger pushes you to act in weird ways. It makes you forget yourself. I was unspeakably hungry; the drinking from the night before seemed to have worsened it. Normally we say bread is for pacifying the kids, but I really needed that bread, even though I had no money. I just stood as if struck dumb. I can't say I was even thinking. Sometimes the brain can grind to a halt and abandon you in a desert of nothingness.

"After hanging around for a while, I looked up only to see the boys watching me intently as they continued buttering their bread. I patted my pockets pretending to look for money that I knew I did not have, and then fake-coughed and pretended I had forgotten my wallet at home. Turning my back and walking away pained me like a chicken being slaughtered with a blunt knife.

"The bread vendors burst into raucous laughter, which annoyed me, for I knew they were laughing at me. I had betrayed myself. If only I had disclosed the truth to them that I had been robbed, they might have felt sorry for me and given me just a slice, or just some crumbs. They, too, were poverty-stricken; one of them had on a tattered shirt that exposed his naked back.

"Walking now became an effort as I was on the last dregs of my strength. I soldiered on anyway and went into the public toilets opposite Herald House. The stench of the toilet. Ooph! It was almost enough to knock me down, especially as I was already dizzy and reeling from hunger. Why do people have to mess up public toilets that way?

"Anyway, I washed my face and sipped a little water to nurse my hangover and to quell my complaining stomach. As I was walking out my stomach gave a loud rumble. The water I had sipped resulted in a painful knot in my stomach. I slumped and sat on a wet patch without even noticing the wetness. My whole mind was terrorized by the pain in my stomach. I got up, the bottom of my pants all wet, and struggled to a park bench, where I sat for a while, head bowed. When I eventually stood up most people were already at work and the city had become a beehive. Slowly I made my way to the Ministry of Education offices. Though they were open, the person processing my papers was away. It made me feel dog-tired.

"'Even if he had been here, you would still need to go to the Salary Services Bureau for approval after we finished processing your papers. Try next week. It seems he went to a funeral.' She spoke looking at me with a 'get lost' attitude.

"Such rude people, who probably got their jobs corruptly, are such a pain. Her attitude stank. I almost spat in her face but managed to restrain myself.

"I left head bowed, weighed down by my thoughts, and crossed the road to the Parliament side. A sparkling-white Mercedes-Benz came to a halt before me. One of the new Mercs with double headlights on either side. The chauffeur came round to open the door for his passenger. Do you know who the passenger was? It was Comrade Garanowako, whom we called Vadzvanyiriri Imbwa—oppressors are dogs. All my sadness melted away and my heart danced with joy.

"'Vadzvanyiriri Imbwa! Is that really you?' I rushed to embrace him. He glared at me like someone seeing vomit on his spotless suit. He tried to get back into his car but only managed to lean against it.

"'Chef Garanowako, do you remember me? I'm Comrade Hamundigone. We trained together at Tete, then we operated together in the Chesa area of Mount Darwin.'

"'Hey driver, get security to remove this person.' That's all he said as he strode to Parliament.

"'But . . .'

"Why did I even bother trying to explain myself? What could I possibly hope to achieve? Did Peter not deny Jesus—not once but thrice? Yes, the very Jesus he had been spending all his time with calling him master? Security dragged and dumped me on Second Street, far away from Parliament, where we nutters are not welcome, even though the place itself is riddled with lunatics.

"I set off toward my daughter Cleodia's workplace. You aren't the only ones who are parents, you know. I too have a daughter, though her mother is dead. She no longer wants to see me, but I had no choice but to go to her. I was sure that she would not let me starve. I went to the bank where she worked, only to be told that she was attending a training course out of town. This left me confounded, with nothing to do but slink out of those cold mortuary-like offices like a thieving dog.

"I started walking aimlessly, hoping to see a familiar face on the streets of Harare. I racked the muck in my brain, trying to think of anyone I could go to for help. After deliberating for a while, I realized that I hardly knew anyone else in Harare apart from my elder brother, Mukoma Ruka. He works at one of those places where you can't just pitch up—you could easily end up in jail. Also he is often away. I could have walked to his home but his wife is rather forbidding, somewhat like a thorny plant. That's why I don't go to his home. All my sisters live in Chitungwiza. I had planned to sleep at Maud's house the day before. I am told that she is very unwell, although I have yet to see her. Mukoma Ruka never visits his folks, so I doubt he knows about her illness.

"I didn't know what to do. I stood around on First Street still hoping for a familiar face but none came. You know when you are avoiding certain people you will doubtlessly bump into them. When you need them, you come across strange faces you have only seen in your dreams.

"I briefly thought about stopping any passerby to explain my suffering, but I was unwilling to turn myself into a beggar. I know all about Harare people and their behavior. They want to act like Americans who have no time for others. You'll see them walking and talking into their cell phones, some of which don't even work. That's what madness does!

"As I wandered back to Africa Unity Square I passed a little bakery along George Silundika Avenue. There were loaves and buns on display in the window. Some people are surely insane.

Imagine displaying bread as window dressing while others are starving to death. Surely if that's not witchery, then I don't know what is. I heard my stomach bellowing like a bull that had knocked down its kraal. Do you know that hunger is more intoxicating than that strong brew, skokiaan? I almost walked in and begged the Indian shopkeeper to give me bread, but I stopped for fear of embarrassing myself. Indians can be arrogant, since they see themselves as almost white. Neediness is simply vile, my friends.

"As I was crossing Second Street, I was nearly run over by a green bus from Domboshava being driven by a white-haired man. His passengers united in scolding me from the windows but I was too weak to reply. Some with deformed faces pressed against the windows, one saying, 'He's mad. Can't you see the way he is dressed and the way he walks?'

"How can one tell a man is mad without even talking to him? Really, people! I left the road and went to find a park bench to sit on, but they were all full of unemployed people tired of looking for jobs. After wandering around dodging people lying on the grass, I found a shady spot near two women who chatted as they did their knitting. Because it was hot I took off my jacket and made it into a pillow and lay down. I watched with envy ants go about their business and idly listened to the women's chatter.

"'That child is my burden. How many fatherless children? She's had five already,' she sighed.

"'And do you accept that?' the other woman asked in shock.

"'What can I do, really? She comes home when she is pregnant, then sneaks away leaving me another baby to look after, only to come back pregnant again.'

"The other woman stopped knitting and said, 'No problem, get her sterilized.'

"'Does she even listen to me? Does she respect me? She's hell on earth, I tell you. She yells at me. To be honest, I don't blame those who have terminated pregnancies.'

"'Now if she carries on that way you'll be stuck with those kids by yourself after she has died of AIDS.'

"'Tell me about it. She's lying sick at home right now. She needs to eat, her kids need to eat, they need soap and clothes. It's all too much for me.'

"The women carried on until I fell asleep around noon only to wake up at dusk. I think I must have died during that time. When I woke up, the park was deserted. Initially I felt confused to find myself having slept outdoors. There were marks on my neck and hands from sleeping on the grass. My mouth tasted like cardboard. I was no longer myself, probably some disorienting spirit had entered into me.

"I tried to pick up my jacket and missed it as I stumbled. I tried to laugh at myself but what I was feeling led to self-pity. The hunger was now a real pain, like a hot brick in my belly. I decided to go to the bins, where I had often seen people in search of food. Shyness is a luxury for the well-fed, not for those who feel the way I was feeling. It was better to search the bins then because nobody would know me in the dark. I staggered to a bench like someone who had drunk an overnight brew, then sat down. The silence and emptiness of the park was eerie. The trees overhead creaked every time the wind blew as if they were in pain. I put on my jacket and sat for a while to clear my head and to come back to my senses. Advertising signs were flashing on and off as if it were a crime that night time had arrived.

"I was silent for a bit, trying to listen to my thoughts and go where they refused to go. I was startled by the bells of the Anglican Cathedral when they started pealing in a way that jarred my nerves. I thrust my head between my knees so as not to hear the bells. By the time they had quietened, I had tears in my eyes and my head was throbbing as if my brain were being pulled out by the roots. Everything had become blurred. I wiped my eyes and sat looking at Nelson Mandela Avenue.

"It is more meaningful to name a street after Mandela because it is relevant to us, unlike Baker. Baker, one of those poverty-stricken Brits who came here to hunt our elephants and escape from the poverty back home. I started to consider Mandela. If only he would walk down this street named after him he would see me and realize that I am not mad. Maybe he would give me a job, or even buy me some sadza at the Meikles Hotel. Maybe he would give me a medal for fighting in the war and tell me that I was a hero like everyone else who fought in the war. People would be awed to see me walk hand in hand with Mandela, with him saying to me, 'Don't call me Mr. Mandela, I am Nelson.' At Meikles we would meet your chefs wanting to speak to Mandela but he would say, 'Not now, I am talking to an important man—Hamundigone.' But would Mandela be able to say my name? I would probably tell him my first name even if it was too hard for him to say. Could he say Pururudzai? He could try, so long as I understood what he was saying.

"I was wrenched out of my reverie by a young man who came to sit on the bench next to me. He wore a white suit. Before sitting down, he cleaned the bench with a tissue from his pocket. He glanced at his watch as he sat down, reminding me of my own watch. I looked at it and saw that it was twelve minutes to seven. The young man in his white suit coughed and I glanced at him. He had a neat haircut and carried a little red flower. Next to him he had placed a small bag. For a moment I entertained the idea that the bag might contain food, but then I realized that he was hardly the type to carry food around. His type dines at Chicken Inn and Nando's. I wanted to talk to him, but the way he was looking this way and that, like someone seeking a bush in a concealed place to safely relieve himself, showed me we had nothing in common. He was obviously waiting for a girl, whom, I suspected, was due to arrive at seven. I examined him; he had a pouting mouth and an earring in one ear.

"'Do you have any tobacco, young man?' I don't even know why I asked that question.

"'Sorry, I do not smoke.'

"He spoke in a too refined English tone and looked away. He was like a rusty piece of sheet metal fallen from the top of a chicken run to be thrown on the rubbish dump. That's how I saw him.

"'No, not cigarettes, I mean bute,' I answered the talking rusty metal sheet.

"'What's bute? Oh you mean snuff? That's a disgusting habit. Do you mean to tell me there are still people using that in this day and age?'

"I did not answer. I thought I saw an angel above the Anglican Cathedral. That's how a hungry person sees things. That's what I thought I saw, sitting in the park next to a rusty sheet of metal.

"I laughed to myself, and the young man looked at me. Perhaps he thought I was laughing at him for being a useless piece of rusty metal or else that I was mad. So I said to him, 'Are you waiting for your girlfriend?'

"'I'm waiting for my boyfriend.'

"Being starved, I thought I had not heard him correctly, so I said, 'Girls are seldom punctual. What time are you supposed to meet?'

"'I said my boyfriend, not girlfriend!'

"He had a nauseating voice that sounded like urine tinkling into a chamber pot.

"'Are you not a boy?' My voice no longer sounded like my own.

"'What is wrong with you people?' he exclaimed, getting up.

"I thought that maybe hunger was driving me mad in making me see a girl like a boy. I just didn't understand it. He walked away and got into a car that had stopped on the other side of Nelson Mandela Avenue, next to the Anglican Cathedral. I saw him kissing the man waiting in the car right on the lips before taking off. This left me with an even greater headache than before, as if someone had spread red-hot coals in my head to bake flatbread.

"It was only after he had gone that I realized that he had left his bag behind. I was tempted to open it and see what was inside but was afraid he would come back for it. I did not want to stay on that bench as I was starting to see more angels on top of the cathedral. I made my way down Nelson Mandela Avenue toward First Street. When I got to Steers on First Street, I abandoned the idea of rummaging in the bins for food because of the large number of people buying food inside and others who were arriving by car. I sat down weakly, leaning against the wall. The flashing lights made me dizzy and nauseous, not that I had anything in me to throw up. I didn't know what was happening to my body.

"While I was struggling with my hunger, a young woman walking with her boyfriend took one bite from a hamburger and tossed it into a bin saying that it had a 'funny taste.' I felt as if I were the one she had thrown into the bin. By the time I got to the bin the street kids had already converged on it. I walked past with a painful heart. I don't even know how I was still walking as I no longer had any strength. I was floating. The world had locked itself behind steel doors with me standing outside knocking in vain.

"I wandered toward OK on First Street, thinking how I had truly become a hobo. Still, I could not understand what those who thought me mad could possibly have seen in me. I pondered this till all I could see before my eyes was darkness. I decided not to burden myself with such heavy thoughts. Though I almost fell, I managed somehow to keep going. I walked down First Street, not a great distance, but I felt as though I was climbing the stairs to heaven. By the time I began walking down Jason Moyo Street I had no fear or shame left. As soon as I got to the bin outside the takeout on Inez Terrace, I immediately stuck my head inside it without even bothering to check if there might be anyone around who knew me. I've never come across a bin as sweet smelling as that one. I found a burger roll and immediately gobbled it up. While still chewing I continued searching and found a few lettuce leaves. I felt them quickly to make sure there were no bits of broken glass and popped them into my mouth. I began to feel a bit more alive. Even the war songs that had started sounding in my head became silent. I could now hear the sounds of the city around me. I sighed in relief and broke a sweat. While my head was still inside the bin, searching for more food, I was suddenly kicked in the belly. My belly tightened with pain and I fell together with the bin. It rolled away, scattering its contents everywhere. As I got up I found myself surrounded by boys—street kids. These kids were vicious like Shaka the Zulu's impis. They dragged me into an alleyway.

"'Who gave you the right to eat from Thomas's bin?' a little skinny boy asked me.

"'What are you saying, little brother?'

"'Old man, you are an idiot. Everyone knows that this bin is Thomas's. If it is touched before he has eaten someone dies.'

"'Who's Thomas?'

"'He's our boss.'

"I could hardly see these boys' faces owing to the darkness in the alleyway. Thomas came running accompanied by three younger boys, making them seven in all. Thomas was a big boy and he immediately dragged me to where it was darker. His hands were hard as planks. I don't know what he used to hit me with, but I was rescued by some passing policemen. I slept at the charge office, where I saw policemen quarreling over dagga that they had confiscated. Imagine. It is—"

"Tickets please. I'll give you your change now if I still owe you," the conductor interrupted the teacher's tale.

"Are we in Harare already? This place is something else," the teacher said.

"So did the government give you your money, my son?" an elderly woman asked.

"Which money, amai? For fighting in the liberation war? Not yet. I am still waiting. Some have been given compensation three times. They doubt if I was a liberation fighter for real. They are still checking their files for my name. I tell them that the bullet scars on my back should be proof enough. If it would not upset you, I could show you. There's nothing for me, amai."

"I meant the pension you were traveling to get in Harare," the elderly woman clarified.

"I did eventually get it. But it's not good to get your pension while you are still able to work and not yet old. There are some people I know, I think you might know some from your area, who are so old that they no longer think straight, but they still go to work. You can even see that those people are crazy but no one stops them from working. They only bully poor helpless people like me. Now that can only be madness. Nothing else."

"Ah-h, are we in Harare already?" one woman asked, rubbing sleep from her eyes.

"We are in Harare, in Marlborough, amai. Had you fallen asleep?" the conductor commented, collecting tickets.

"I fell asleep listening to my son's story about how he almost starved to death in Harare. I did not hear how it ended. I'm coming from a funeral, that's why I'm so tired."

"There are too many deaths these days. If you don't sleep when you get a chance you never do. As for my stories, they are just the mutterings of a madman. I didn't starve to death, although I was almost killed by the street kids. All the same, I am very happy to be back in Harare. I love Harare. I don't like it when people curse those who come to Harare and never go back to their homes." The teacher rubbed his eyes and then continued. "What can they do when Harare is so extraordinary? This Harare is simply fabulous."

Those who had been silently listening to the teacher started laughing.

"So you are laughing? You're actually laughing? I suppose you think that I am drunk. OK, if I am drunk we will see who misses his stop, you or me. Ah, you may laugh, but I'm telling the truth. Mothers, don't let your children come to Harare, they will never return. Never mind, you mothers are in Harare now anyway. Do you think Magumbo would want to return to Zaka after tasting town life? That would not do at all as there are no bright lights in Jerera. Let me reminisce about Mahwinheyi, the girl I was to marry when we were at Nyombwe, but forgot about when I came to Harare." People burst into laughter.

"Well you may laugh, but I loved that girl. Sadly, Harare bewitched me and made me forget her. She should have been the mother of my children. Even worse, I forgot my own mother. I remember the year I went to Kudenga Night Club . . . Hey driver, do you know Kudenga's? Wait, let me tell you. No, I didn't say to stop the vehicle, I'm saying listen up while I tell you. Right, Kudenga is in Hatcliffe. Listening to Simon Chopper Chimbetu singing in that nightclub brought back memories of my mother:

Shirikadzi inochema-chema mwana wangu dangwe nagotwe,
Kana waenda kuchirungu, ndinyorerewo tsamba,
Ndinyorerewo ndizive wakadini, ndinyorerewo ndizive unofara.

The widow sobs, my one and only child,
If you go to the city, write to me,
Write to me so I know how you are, write so I know you are well.

"This Harare is formidable. It's bizarre, like the gun I used to tote in the war when I was still a comrade. Comrade who? Hamundigone. Who ran away from my gun? The enemy. Unfortunately I am no longer a comrade because every other lizard is now calling itself comrade.

"Let me decide what to do now that I am in Harare. I have two sisters here in Harare and a brother. Mukoma Ruka is here in Harare but I will not set foot in his house. I may end up getting shot. Added to that, I don't want to go where I'll be miserable and not able to laugh freely because they want to be British. So I'll go to one of my sisters in Chitungwiza.

"Yet Chitungwiza is not Harare. There are cattle there so it is rural. Do I go to Mai Jazz's or Mai Reuben's? Mai Jazz talks too much. Have you ever seen her? Her mouth has aged too fast and she can't spend a day without shouting at someone. She must have a postgraduate degree in popotology. Some people are impossible. If only it were just her, but the daughter Heaven is worse. As for Maud, the mother of Reuben, it is her I have come to see. The telegram said she is so sick that if I don't come quickly I will find her dead. This is terrible. What is really going on? I am tired of all these deaths. The sickness and dying is simply too much. Almost like a competition." He stopped talking for a while and looked out of the window.

"Yeah, there is the University of Zimbabwe, the pinnacle of education. I did my graduate certificate in education there." He pointed toward the University of Zimbabwe.

"Just imagine with all that education and knowledge, someone is sent to give me a letter saying stop teaching because you are mad! It's all nonsense, madness." He paused as though expecting a response, then shook his head.

"This is Second Street and your president lives behind it, over there. Across there is the golf course, for the wealthy, not poor beggars like us. Driver, do you know how much one golf club costs? I won't tell you. Go and find out for homework and tell me tomorrow. Look at those bright lights up ahead. Harare is beautiful. Oh look, even you, Mai Kambanje, have permed hair. So what problems can you possibly have? Don't forget to go back kumusha to do your farming though. Because I myself, the president of Harare, am tired of it. Harare is worthless. Like bubblegum that has lost its flavor and just wastes your energy in chewing. If I could just find a better place, if such a place exists, I would flee there. Have you ever seen a person who could run away from his own home, like birds that abandon their own nests once they become too messed up? That's what I want to do. I would be glad to find a place to slip away to, far away from Harare. Far away indeed from this madness. This madness, which sees the lunacy in others while refusing to acknowledge its own lunacy."

No one spoke.

"Driver, Harare scares me, my brother. It frightens me to imagine that this is life. Once I ran away as far as I could, but found I was missing Harare the way it is. Sometimes I feel Harare is a pain like being rejected by your own child, unlike a girlfriend who had never been kin in the first place. Mothers, have any of you ever been rejected by a child you bore and nursed and cared for? It hurts badly. My daughter Cleodia rejected me. Anyway, it doesn't matter anymore—that is my fate. If only—"

"Please drop me off after Tongogara," whined the girl at whom the teacher had previously shouted.

"Is this where you live or have you come to work?" the teacher asked.

She ignored the teacher's question.

"Well then, do your work well, young lady, but please do not destroy the country. Also learn to speak properly not through the nose as though you have a cold. This chinozi of yours is disgusting," the teacher called out as she was disembarking.

"Pfutseki, you're as ugly as a baboon that has eaten sour fruit. What has my job or the way I talk got to do with you? I make my money tax-free and, unlike you, no one can fire me. I am my own boss. And I'm not mad like you!"

"You think you're your own boss? Wait and see, AIDS will surely find you," retorted the teacher.

"You can go to hell. You are really crazy. You scum of the earth," the girl responded.

"Ha, I'm scum am I? What about you? There really are many of us crazies for sure." The teacher spoke as the kombi took off.

"I'm surprised she actually speaks Shona. It sounded to me like a white person trying to speak our language," said an elderly man with glasses as thick as the base of a Coca-Cola bottle.

Eyeing the miniskirt-clad girls standing along Second Street, the conductor said, "Mothers, if you didn't know it, I had already realized what sort this girl is. She has come all the way to Harare to kill people. She's a whore, that's what. They loiter in wait for clients here on Second Street. Not my type, but for those who can afford to pay a lot of money."

"Let these people of darkness finish each other off. Why do you suppose they only move at night? They are evil. Am I lying, driver, my bro'?" the teacher said, as he too peered out of the window.

"Hmm. Folks, this is Sodom and Gomorrah. These people can't even see how others are dying of AIDS." The driver spoke his mind for the first time since leaving Bindura.

"Harare is a snake hiding in the pocket, it's no longer safe, my son," spoke a woman with a black headscarf.

"Ah, Harare has always been like this, unsafe. In the dark of the night Harare is a garishly painted whore. She wears a multicolored face of lights to lure away people's money. Money! Money is bloody, good people, no different from the war we fought to get rid of the enemy. It's bloody. Harare is shameless do you know—and heartless. It is immoral like a plate that you dish out on even though it has not been washed. If only I had time, I would tell you what I saw the following morning when I left the charge office. Harare! I fear Harare. It fills me with dread, like a hen wanting to fight a cockerel but knowing full well it could easily end up in a pot with tomatoes and onions. Ooh, thinking of chicken makes me hungry. Does anyone have any chicken to give me?" the teacher asked, licking his lips.

"I've no chicken, my son, but here are some roasted peanuts," the woman with the black headscarf offered, handing him peanuts tied up in a small plastic bag.

"Thank you, my mother, carer of orphans." The teacher gave thanks, clapping his hands.

"Try them, they are not well matured, the rains stopped early this year," she commented, shutting her bag.

"There is no way I could eat them here. I can see from the conductor's eyes that he wants some, so I'll put them away in my pocket." The people laughed as the teacher put the peanuts into his trouser pocket.

"Conductor, if they are not paying you enough money to buy yourself food, what are you killing yourself for, my brother? If they are not giving you enough for sadza, clothing and rent, then you should take some of that money when you finish your shift, because no one is coming to save you. There's no promotion for you, sonny. Maybe one day you'll become a driver? This black employer you work for, I bet you he has twenty kombis and eats to excess, but you, my brother, are the toiler. Never fear, all this abuse will come to an end, just give it time."

He took out his filthy handkerchief to wipe the sweat gleaming on his face and resumed his discourse on Harare.

"Harare. It's said they don't sleep in Harare. That's not a lie. No one sleeps in Harare and everything's there. If you can't see it, you're going blind, get glasses. Drunks, the religious, the adulterous, celebration partygoers, gay association members, political party members, street kids, moviegoers, thugs, everything. Ah,

Harare destroys my head like a spade shoveling manure. I don't understand it, it's corrupt, it stinks, but I love it. I love it the way kids love the sound of the ice cream vendor's bell. Have you ever seen them chasing the ice cream tricycle? The problem is that Harare youths are too accustomed to delicacies. Anyway, it's not their fault; nice things are made to be eaten.

"You can't compete with Harare. Let it be. Here's what I think. Bus driver, when we get to the terminus, I want to go back with you to Bindura. No more Harare. Its breast has nursed some to maturity, but its graves for the young outnumber those reaching a ripe old age by far. A character in a novel I once taught said, 'Harare is a great ancestral spirit.' What he never explains is what kind of beer or invocation this mighty spirit requires. When my students wanted to know about Harare, I told them to come and see for themselves, but to remember that it may not actually be ours since it was built by white men before we left our rural homes to come and stay and work here. When we found it agreeable, we clipped the wings that had brought us here from our rural homes and became its denizens. Anyway, the majority of people in Harare are black and there's nothing new because even Salisbury found Harare here already. Let's go driver, but don't forget to leave me at the Terreskane Hotel!" He burst out laughing.

"You people are all listening to me—do you think I'm sane? These are but the ramblings of a lunatic—let them be. But whoever calls me a lunatic—watch out. You lunatics! I'm dropping off at the Main Post Office. Comrades, see you."

The kombi stopped and the teacher dropped off together with a number of others. They were embraced by the dimly lit streets of Harare.

At the Hospital

Do you know that visiting a hospital to see the sick can end up being terrifying? There are times when you visit someone and carry along fruit and other food they may want to eat. Things will still be OK at that stage. Later, there comes a time when you simply visit the sick to stare at the bare walls in hopelessness. That's when the elders refer to that saying—you may admire your sister's breast, but no matter how arousing it may be, there's not a thing that you as a brother can do about it. There are such visits to the hospital, where your hope gets sick like the patient you are visiting. The patient will no longer be eating, talking, or even opening their eyes. Like your hope, they will be breathing very faintly. If you feel their hand, it will be weak and frighteningly cool. Even the drip will no longer be working as it should. When you look at the needle stuck in skin and bone, you actually feel the pain as if it were stuck in your own skin and bone. Things can be like that. In such times you feel as if death is among the visitors at the hospital bedside. A dreadful gloominess settles over the whole scene.

I no longer wanted to come and see Maud. I did not feel there was any hope of life; we were just waiting for death to swing his scythe. Hospital visiting time is not very long, just one hour, but that hour can feel like a month. It's so scary to realize that a person can dwindle to that size in so short a time. When I got home yesterday I had no appetite at all, in fact the mere smell of food grated on me.

I arrived twenty minutes into visiting time. I had not come to the lunch visit, not that I was busy, but the hospital visits and Maud's condition had just become unbearable. The situation weighed me down as does a thick woolen jersey in the rain. In my heart I felt I had seen enough and was unwilling to see anymore. I was overwhelmed.

I thought I would find other visitors there. The hard thing about coming to visit a person who is no longer able to talk is that it's you, the visitors, who have to make conversation among yourselves. But the talking doesn't go very far. You ask how the others are, then you ask those who arrived early, "Did she eat today, did she say anything today?" After that you just stand there and gaze at her lying in her bed. You agonize, wondering if she will ever get up and walk again. Your thoughts become a punishment.

I found her mother frozen in her seat gazing where her daughter lay, never blinking or moving. The old woman looked grim like a spirit medium. Her thoughts and what I could see in her eyes seemed as terrifying as John's visions in the Book of Revelation. I almost did not recognize her because, apart from her staring eyes, her face was gray and drawn as if she had been assaulted by ghosts. Her eyes were sunken and black. They looked like those caves full of mystery, which they say are sacred because the ancestors are buried there. Those caves are solemn places. At that moment she bowed her head, displaying a faded black headscarf. She seemed to be praying, so I remained at the foot of the bed.

I bent my head to look at the card on which the doctors and nurses had scrawled. The handwriting was illegible, like the tracks of wet ducks, and almost identical, as if written by children of the same parent. I heaved a great sigh. Whether it was fear or tiredness I am not sure—it was a mixture of both, I think. The card was illegible, but they had told me it was pneumonia. It's hard to tell whether it is pneumonia alone or whether it has become like a bicycle overloaded with a lot of things, which is hard to steer or balance. I did not bring anything for her to eat. The way she lay was scary because it was hard to know whether she was living or not.

"How are you, Samanyanga?"

I was startled. Her voice sounded so worn. It was full of unshed tears, full of unhealed wounds. The voice was no longer her own. The other thing that startled me was her use of my totem name. Are there still people in Harare who call one by one's totem? Totem and clan names in Harare are the car you drive, the checkbook and MasterCard you carry, the suits you wear, and the type of cell phone you have. That is what people will know rather than your totem or clan name. The time for those is past. My mind was searching and probing, trying to find meaning in Maud's sickness. Besides, I'm more used to people calling me Bunny, not by my totem the rural way.

"I'm well enough, old lady. How are you?"

"I'm so-so. There's not much I can do. Just waiting and watching that which hovers over us like a flock of vultures." She spoke resignedly, watching the bed where her daughter lay.

"Ah yes, well what else can we do? I have been here for a while, but I thought you were praying, so I kept quiet." I thought to talk about something other than the patient.

"Eish Samanyanga, my head was bowed by the weight of my thoughts; I'm tired and helpless," she said, adjusting her headscarf as if that would help with the mental weight.

I did not want to tell her that she had even raised her head and failed to see me standing by the foot of the bed.

"Have you spoken to her at all?"

"She just opened her eyes briefly when I asked her how she was, that's all."

I felt defeated, and afraid.

"Have Sekuru and the others come?" I asked, looking at the piles of oranges and bananas and other uneaten food.

"Ah, can anyone understand Sekuru Hamundigone? He himself is sick. I can't follow his conversation. It seems to be getting worse since they fired him," she said, sniffing.

"Oh, do you really think so? I don't think Sekuru is really mad because I can follow his ideas. His talk is quite comprehensible. Since he is said to have mental health issues, everyone thinks that is so, including him. You know it is really difficult to convince people that you are sane. That is what I think."

"Eish, I don't know, we'll see. It could be that, because he was in the war, he saw too much blood and it is now haunting him. If only he would agree to go for treatment. I don't know; we'll see where it leads. It's too much to bear considering Maud's situation, and Sekuru Hamundigone. It's just too trying," she said, looking tormented.

"Ambuya, please stop that kind of talk, else you will weigh down the patient with worries on top of her illness." I wanted to take her mind off the issue she persisted in discussing.

"Never mind, Samanyanga, it is but fate. Don't they say all things are already written?" she said, bowing her head. Her headscarf reminded me of the wings of a click beetle from the days I used to herd cattle when I was kumusha. Her eyes were full of tears. I hate to see tears. From the redness of her eyes she couldn't have slept in days.

I did not want to stay too long at the hospital today because my mind was burning with a flame I was trying to douse. You know, it is impossible for me to think that those are the lips I once kissed, lips that once smiled softly. It was better when we could still talk to each other. We could still lie to each other that it was only an ordinary illness, not the big and feared AIDS that has devoured so many. You know, Maud was suddenly taken ill only three weeks ago. Now I fear what ails her could be lurking in me. Why did I ever do it? I had stayed in her house for eleven months and we had been lovers for eight of them. Even though we used condoms, it is not certain that I am not infected. It's hard, I don't know anymore. It's a good thing she couldn't use the contraceptive pill because she was allergic to it, otherwise I would know for sure that I am infected. Still, I can't simply assume that I am safe just because we always used condoms. I'm even scared to go for a blood test. I don't know the condition of the blood flowing in my veins. I'll leave it as it is, maybe I will only know when I get sick. Terrible, horrible life. If only I hadn't done it. Frailty, thy name is human, not woman.

I simply did not have the energy to wait till the end of the visiting hour. Forgetting to say goodbye to Maud's mother, I left the ward. I have only just realized that I did not respond to the greetings of those I met coming into the ward on my way out. I think I saw Mai Heaven, Charity, and others I did not recognize. Too bad if they thought me arrogant, I really cannot face going back to acknowledge them, so I'll see what tomorrow brings.

I went down to my car, my mind refusing to work. I simply sat in the car doing nothing, not even thinking, until it grew dark. In my mind, I saw an empty football stadium with me in the center and no one else. I felt so small. The coldness of sweat pouring from all my pores brought me back to my senses. It was as if I had just awoken from a nightmare. I was filled with fear and at a complete loss. I felt my heart had a gaping hole through which air could flow, whistling like a dzvoti snake.

I don't know. Life is frightening. It is a tangled mass of confusion. Have you ever asked yourself why you exist? Living is fear, anxiety, and ignorance. Life is tears, torment, searching, groping in vessels already emptied. Searching and searching for what? Dembo sang that life is untamable, and its claws are ruthless. It is hard to look forward to a future when all hope has been smashed to bits. I don't know what I am living for. If I knew I would wait in alertness like a dog watching people eat in the hope they will toss a bone its way.

I don't know what I shall do. These days the breasts of nursing mothers are being snatched away from hungry infants when they still want to suckle. Lightning strikes seeds even before they are sown. It is meaningless. If it means anything, clear eyes are needed to see it. Is it perhaps the end? I would not doubt it.

I started the car and drove off with no idea as to where I was going.

Bunny

There are certain things that happen in life, and only you and the person you were with at the time know exactly what happened. Things like the time your wife thought you had a two-day conference in Victoria Falls while you were somewhere else doing something else. Such lies may be hard to forget and will forever cook your mind. They are like a small stone that gets into your shoe when you are in a hurry to get somewhere and don't want to waste time by stopping to get it out, even though it makes it harder for you to walk fast.

People say a problem shared is a problem halved. It could be true. There are some problems that I discuss with my mates and they get sorted out fast. You realize that the ancients knew about life when they stated that whatever issue is presented before the village council will surely be solved. If you tell others about your problem, they will thrash it out till they separate the chaff from the grain. But there are some problems, like this particular one, which are not suitable for sharing. We may share problems, but everyone has a little private nook in their life known only to themselves. Even with that girlfriend of yours, the one who gives you sleepless nights, who makes your heart dance and who has told you that you are the only one and her life is an open book to you, she has her own little nook that she will never tell you about. It could be about something that happened in her childhood—it will ever remain her secret. Don't you know about Magi's friend Kundai, who was married to Titus for five years before they divorced? They had two kids. We all thought these were Kundai and Titus's kids but were surprised after the divorce to hear that Kundai had refused to leave the children with Titus because he was not the father. It happens! None of us knew about that little nook, which Kundai hid for the five years she was married to Titus. That's the way the game of life goes, all of us play it but some cheat and keep secrets as wide as streets.

Even the married guys say there are secrets that must never get to their wives. People are often shocked at funerals when the children of the deceased are asked to stand up. And, oh boy! Some children, even older than the ones you have always known, stand up. Or when someone dies and all sorts of people crawl out of the woodwork claiming entitlement to the deceased's estate. You see a woman claiming to be the wife of the deceased and that he even paid lobola to formalize the marriage. Such news makes the official widow so overburdened by the mental agony of it all that she falls sick. Only widows with a civil or church marriage preceding these other so-called marriages will be protected. These things happen; after all only the shoe knows how many holes there are in the sock.

I've lost a lot of weight these days because of the issue of Maud. It's not only the weight I've lost; I can no longer enjoy myself even when I am with my mates. Even beer has lost its taste; it has become brackish like borehole water from some far-flung village in the back of beyond. It is as awful as muteyo—that medicine used to pick out the witch from a crowd. It is harder than the hard times Simon Chimbetu sang about. At such tough times the boys say one does not so much sweat but steam. They say if you find yourself just sweating, then things are still OK. Personally, I am in a really tight spot, a stewpot, but I can't discuss it with anyone. This is my own little nook.

It is hard for me to see how she enticed me, or comprehend why she presented me with such temptation. I don't know. I appreciated that people can be evil when I realized that a gun was made primarily for shooting other people, not just anyplace but in the head. If you shoot someone in the leg and they get away, the next time they may shoot you in the head because you let them go. It's the same thing with a snake; if you don't crush its head it will lunge at you. A human gives birth to you, but you can be killed by a human and it would be a human who buries you by piling up rocks over the coffin to ensure that you can never rise again. A human! Animals are better because their behavior is predictable; a human is totally unpredictable.

Isn't that the reason why Maud's brother, the teacher, when he saw people eyeing him outside the hospital after a visit, said, "People! I'm livid, I'm furious like an injured buffalo. But I've not yet reached the limit. I am more afraid of a human being than I am afraid of a lion because I know that a lion will eat me. It is its nature and there's nothing mysterious about that. I'm more afraid of my own relatives than witches and sorcerers because I expect sorcerers to possess deadly magic potions. My relatives look at me and smile as though they love me like a baby. What are you afraid of and why do you fight me? Isn't it that you have all been told that I am mad and that's what you see?" If you want to know the depth of human evilness, buy *Kwayedza* and read for yourself the things people do.

Looking at it carefully, being a lodger is to accept being in a vulnerable situation. Your life is entirely in another's hands. Being a lodger is no different from a job one gets as a result of being a good-looking woman. When the man who gave the woman the job comes to claim a reward for the favor he has done, it takes a morally upright woman to resist. With the hardships and poverty prevailing today, many are putting their marriages on the line to get jobs. And when someone has given you a job, it's not that different from someone who has given you a room to rent. They will toy with you. That has been my experience. I think when that woman saw me looking for rooms to rent, she must have said to herself, "Lucky me, I've found myself a boyfriend." I never suspected her at the time, I just felt that she was a trifle overfriendly. I had heard from my mates about the rooms to rent in Zengeza 3. My pals told me that the landlady was still a young woman and presentable too. From the way they spoke I gathered that there was something that they wanted me to find out for myself. You know how it is with the guys. I went twice to Zengeza 3 looking for Maud, only to find the housemaid with a young child who was not yet of school-going age.

The bachelor flat I rented in Glen Norah no longer suited me. Though bachelor flats are called that, they are not really suitable for a bachelor who wants something a bit more spacious. I was also looking forward to going to live in Zengeza, given that I had lots of friends in Fiyo and I wanted to get away from them. Zengeza was too distant for us to see each other often. Sometimes if you have too many friends you do not make progress, particularly if the friends are like mine who are always thinking of beer and weddings. "Wedding" is a term they use to refer to any kind of revelry. Never mind that the event is in Gweru and you are in Harare, you go. Or they might suddenly say let's go and watch Oliver Mtukudzi perform in Sakubva Stadium in Mutare. Most of the time it was a matter of agreeing on spontaneous and irrational stuff, stuff that you later regret. This often happened to me and I would later say to myself, when it was too late, if only I had refused. The boys then tell you that "if only" is a mad man's philosophy. The life of youths in Harare is much like the heavily polluted Mukuvisi River.

It was better in Zengeza because there were some guys that I got on with, both in Seke Unit K and Zengeza, though not as many as in Fiyo. My younger brother Vincent was in Seke Unit D. Even though we did not really get along, blood ties are blood ties and can't be washed away with soap. One of my Zengeza guys told me how fine the lodgings were and this aroused my interest. However, what they seemed to most want was for me to see the beauty of the landlady. I was not interested in this, since I had my own girl, Lorna, at Solusi University in the back of beyond. Though she used to scold me about my lifestyle with the Fiyo boys in pursuit of beer and weddings, she still loved me and I loved her.

I almost did not bother asking about the lodgings, as many days had elapsed from the time I first heard about them. You know how it is in the ghetto, many of the lodgings aren't vacant for long. I had been impressed by what my friends had told me about Maud's place, so I kept considering it. They said the place was fenced and well kept, and the lodgings were a self-contained section at the back of the house, built with letting them out in mind. The rooms were scarcely visible from the road, only a bit of the roof could be seen. The lodgings consisted of two large rooms plus a bathroom-cum-toilet. It seemed to be my dream place. There are no constant conflicts with the house owners in such a place. You will never have a situation where you are told "Mukoma, baba says can you come out of the shower," when you have just lathered your hair. Once this has been said you have to leave the shower immediately, never mind the lather in your hair or in your eyes—that is your own lookout because the landlord is the boss.

Another thing that doesn't sit well with me is having to greet the landlord politely in acknowledgment that he is the property owner. Such issues make me madder than someone who has smoked dagga from Mutoko, which I have heard can make one crazy high. True, people must greet each other, but it becomes exaggerated in the case of lodgers. It can become an issue that can lead to your eviction if the landlord thinks you are disrespectful. Don't you know that Sanchez, Vincent's commuter omnibus driver friend, was evicted from his lodgings without notice for hitting the landlord's dog? The dog had entered Sanchez's room and eaten the uncooked meat on the table.

When Sanchez found it licking its chops, he whacked it and the house owner told him to take a walk. He said you should not have hit my dog, you should have waited for me and told me what my dog had done, and then I would have compensated you. When he tried to appeal, the landlord said to him, I might have forgiven your lapse if you greeted me every morning and gave me free rides in your kombi. Harare is brutal. All the same, a dog ought to be disciplined by its owner. If it ever does what this one did then it should be thoroughly beaten. Only there are some people for whom their cat or dog is as lovable as their own child, maybe more. Who knows, maybe it is we who are insane; as Hamundigone is wont to say, the crazy are difficult to identify. Imagine such behavior. As my sister Magi often says, "What kind of thing is that?" or else she says, "Just where are you losing it?"

So, anyway, I went to the place and was fortunate enough to find the landlady there. And found the lodgings still vacant. So she asked me for my payslip, saying that she wanted to verify my ability to pay the rent.

"Excuse me, ma'am. Do you suppose that I would come looking for lodgings that I was unable to pay for?" I asked, astonished at the request. I had been a lodger in many places before and I had friends who were lodgers, but no one had ever mentioned showing the landlady a payslip.

"Eish, brother, don't act as if you don't know how people behave in Harare. Do you want me to go through a history of my former lodgers? People are a problem and you know it. I have no husband and, besides going to South Africa to buy stuff for my market stall, I have no other source of income. So I want someone who can pay my rent without any problems."

I silently thought to myself, this woman is a motormouth. "Yes, I hear you but—" I wanted to explain to her that I had never heard such a thing before but scarcely got a chance.

"Do you want the lodgings, my brother . . . by the way, what's your name?" she asked, head tilted as she helped her maid undo the braids in her hair.

"Bunny," I answered, my mouth suddenly gone dry.

"Why, you have a nice name. I love Bugs Bunny cartoons on TV. So what do you say? Let's get this over with, I want to shampoo my hair." She was almost finished with the braids in her hair and didn't seem to be interested in me.

I dislike being compared to or seen as a cartoon. However, I decided that it didn't matter since I really needed the lodgings. Hamundigone compares such a situation to a sick person who craves roast locust so much that he will hang on to one of its legs while it is roasting to make sure it doesn't fall into the fire.

"Yeah, I do want the rooms, it's just—" I was cut short. She talked too much, just like my sister Magi.

"You don't want to show anyone your payslip because they will see that you have stacks of money, right?"

"No, it's not that. Let me check in my briefcase to see if, by chance, I have one. I don't usually carry one as I don't think it's important."

Digging around papers in a briefcase can be a bother. I usually get the payslips from our salaries office and put them away or tear them up. After all, what do they matter? Everyone knows what they earn and, besides, it's finished long before one even begins spending. While going through all the papers, I was startled to come across a letter that I had forgotten about and I said to myself, I must reply to that letter when I get home. While I have accommodation problems in town, the Old Man, at our rural home, needs money to pay taxes for his cattle and to pay the herdboy. I would hate a repeat of what happened one time when the Old Man just pitched up unexpectedly. He found me sitting outdoors with my friends, drinking. He fumed at me. It took my friend Munya, one of my drinking mates, to cool the situation down by giving the Old Man $500. The Old Man did not even bother to come into the house; he turned right around and went back kumusha. He even refused to be taken to Mbare, saying, "Where will you find money for fuel to take me there when you claim to not have any?" We lost our appetites and didn't drink much after he left.

Ah, money issues, so long as I'm not the Minister of Finance, I said to myself after I found the payslip and closed the briefcase.

"Here's a payslip."

"Right. Ooh, I see you have lots of it. So my $1,000 rent will not be difficult to pay, right? You need to make a $1,000 deposit. This deposit will be returned to you should you decide to leave the lodgings, on condition that you have not broken any of my windows."

"I don't have any cash on me, is it OK if I write a check? I really want the place," I said with mixed feelings. I was happy to have found a place but was worried that she seemed difficult and could refuse my check.

"No problem, as long as your check does not bounce. I am going to cash it tomorrow."

"It's OK, it won't bounce," I said happily, retrieving my payslip from her glass table.

Her house was well appointed. The carpet, the sofas, and the brass room divider were stunning. As for the radio, it had a CD compartment. Very few people in the ghetto have radios with CDs. Everything about the decor was beautiful. I think she was well off by ghetto standards.

"So when did you say you will move in?" she asked, picking off fibers of hair extensions that had fallen on her jersey.

"I can come at the weekend, when I have asked for a car from work," I said, without thinking that the issue of a car would be so gratifying to her.

"You have a car! So where will you park it? I ask for fear that it might be stolen and you might blame me. I have no security for your car. Anyway, let me give you the keys to your rooms and the gate. Oh, by the way, my name is Maud or Mai Reuben or Mrs. Chamboko. As I told you earlier, my husband passed away last year from high blood pressure, so I do not mind what you call me. Do you mind if I call you Bunny rather than bothering with mukoma?" she asked, changing her manner of speaking in a way that left me bemused. I did not answer at once, I kept silent as if considering her question, then said, "Ah no, it does not matter, all my friends call me Bunny and, besides, that's my name."

"So Bunny, we can discuss the outstanding issues when you

come at the weekend. I'm not difficult and I am not cruel like other landlords and landladies. So we'll see you when you come; I'll be here this weekend. But who cleans and polishes your veranda for you? Anyway never mind, we'll talk about it, won't we?"

That was my first meeting with Maud, who became my lover. I had no plans in mind for her and did not suspect her of anything, as I had clearly told her that I had a fiancée. She seduced me. If I had known how Joseph managed Potiphar's wife, I would have done the same. But there are certain situations where there's no escaping.

University of Zimbabwe—Magi

People do not understand that being raped muddies your life. People think that because I went with him to Troutbeck Inn I had given him consent. I thought we were just flirting and I never saw this coming.

Bunny never said anything. He was silently brooding, full of bitterness and anguish. I think Bunny is pained because he takes care of all of my baby Rudo's needs. My mother was looking after my baby in the hopes that I would reform, only to have me fall pregnant again. Now Kenny, the boy more my age, whom I wanted to fool into believing that he was responsible, would have none of it when I told him that I was pregnant. How could he shout about it in such a loud voice that the entire corridor would hear? The news has now spread all over the college. The folks here are so interested in scandals and other people's business, not even *Kwayedza* is that bad. Kenny really hurt me, though I should not really take offence since my attempt to trick him into accepting responsibility for someone else's baby was evil. You know a desperate person does desperate things. And then, when it comes to the monster who made me pregnant, he said, "You know I have a wife and children at home so it just won't work, Magi. Just forget about it and let's close the chapter."

So I was the fool who dated a married man. I became the

two-liter mug used for communally drinking the traditional brew in the beer hall, which is then taken home to be used as a chamber pot and a bucket for scrubbing the floor, before returning to the beer hall to be drunk from again. It's not really my fault, because when it all started, he had spiked my drink. You know when you drink alcohol unknowingly you suddenly find yourself in a situation that is hard to get out of. I had made up my mind that I did not want to have another baby. All I wanted from Mangwiro was a good time. I was hoping to eventually find someone that I would truly love so that I could ditch the old man. I just did what every other girl here at college is doing; they have affairs with married men and tell you that they are only looking for money to survive. Many of them deny that they are whores, but the truth is that we all prostitute ourselves. So my story is no different. In fact, I was holding on lightly, knowing that I might have to let go at any time. I can't say I was serious about the relationship. I never wanted to become so intimate with him that we would sleep together. He knew this. Maybe he felt he had spent too much on me in all the places we went. I think that is what made him think of getting me drunk at Troutbeck Inn in Nyanga. I almost told Kundai, but all the girls at college think I am a tart. What they can't see is that I really try to have steady relationships with unmarried young men, but they don't work out. I really try; no one enjoys a life of being forever on the road without a destination. You need a station where you can rest. If only I had known, I would have gone to a convent and become a nun. Nothing ever works for me. As soon as I start to think something good is about to happen a worm comes from somewhere to spoil the lot.

Another person who really hurt me was Jonathan, my former boyfriend, who was a medical student when he snubbed me because of the degree I was studying. What a reason! And here I was thinking I had found my very own man. Going out with someone for a year and seven months is not a joke. You know it is really painful, you think you have found someone who loves you as much as you love him, while he is not being straight with you. All those sweet words. It hurts. It hurts you and makes you feel envious when other people's relationships work out while yours don't. I ask myself what my crime on earth is and what sin I have committed against God. Why, I even tried going to church but it simply didn't work. You just feel like a hypocrite. Are arranged relationships still viable in this day and age? That does not do at all. People must get involved after studying each other's personalities, not the situation where the pastor says Sister So-and-So I think you and Brother Such-and-Such will have a blessed love. That's ridiculous! I told them I wanted out rather than being forced into a relationship with someone with whom I was not compatible. That's why some people end up having sad families. Because they will just be making do. Love should come from your heart. When you find someone that you really love, you just know.

The trouble that I went through when I was made pregnant by my teacher is not to be repeated. Only things were different then. That man loved me. He was even prepared to marry me, but circumstances stopped him. I think it was just that I panicked. If it had not been known while I was still in school, it would have worked out after I finished writing my exams. Hamundigone, father of my child. It's hard to tell whether it is true that he is now mad.

No one suspected that I could be capable of doing such things. The person who was most furious was my mother. She said that if I had told her earlier she would not have wasted money on educating me. When my father found out, he beat my mother, accusing her of having encouraged me in my wrongdoing. There's nothing so painful as to be beaten for a crime you have not committed. I could not even look into her swollen eyes. What really pained me is the fact that Father did not speak to me. Not once. He simply ignored me.

Now, not a single person will feel sorry for me. I did not tell anyone except my mother that I was pregnant again. My mother must have felt overwhelmed and carelessly told Bunny. I realized that I was on my own when I heard my mother saying, "Magi, the first offence can be forgiven, but now you've given us an unworkable equation, not even with a calculator can we work it out."

Let me go to Kundai's room; if I stay here, I'll surely go mad. I feel it. But is it too late for an abortion? It has been three months now since the rape, and I think I'm going to abort. Let people say whatever they wish, I don't care about it. Only it takes money; backstreet abortions are scary. I'll ask others who have had abortions. There are lots of them at college and they are known. If only I had not told my mother so soon. It was she who wrecked everything by telling Bunny and others. Let me think. But if I explain it properly, I may be able to get Mangwiro arrested for raping me, because so far I'm the one who gets left ditched in the sewer. Mangwiro raped me, that's the truth. This is cruelty like a snake's; it bites something that it cannot even eat. Honestly, some people will not enter heaven. I never imagined that circumstances can, like dough, knead one's life emotionally like this. I have to let it out. I have read about people who only reveal having been raped years down the line. Let me go and talk to Kundai.

Dogs

Honestly, when is this madness going to end? Sekuru Saba bought a whore two dresses and a pair of shoes, but when you see his wife you wonder whether her frightful clothes were taken from a scarecrow or are hand-me-downs from ancient times. But why, Saba? In Harare, this is the way people behave.

I'm not saying that I am the most sensible of people, but I find Sekuru Saba is simply appalling. A prostitute of all things? His wife is always coming to me to beg for money for mealie meal or sugar to make porridge for the baby. At other times, she asks for money to buy penny cools for resale, and yet he gets money to spend on a tart? Only yesterday he came to my home with that bitch. She was huge, like a mountain, with a bust resembling a dairy cow's udder. How can someone come to me in my single room at two in the morning asking for a place to sleep with a tart? If Mai Tanyaradzwa were not his partner, I would have thought that maybe he wanted to marry that huge person he brought to my house. Consider how sweet dreams are at two o'clock in the morning, when you dream that, dressed in white overalls and gumboots, you are walking among multicolored ice popsicles in your own ice cream factory. Sleep can be sweeter than your first kiss from the girl who has been giving you sleepless nights.

So Sekuru Saba coming meant that I would have to leave my bed and go to sleep on the floor. That's where I drew the line. Sekuru Saba alternately tried bluster and sweet talk to persuade me to see things his way, the glowing tip of his cigarette flashing around in the dark all the while.

"Listen Buddy, I've organized myself a nice deal with this woman and if you can't accommodate me then you're really letting me down." He tried to coax me in a mellow voice.

"No, Sekuru, you can't arrange to use my room without my knowledge, that's being too presumptuous."

"My guy, why can't you be understanding?"

"I'll never be understanding because being understanding is for the ZANU supporters, who chant slogans like 'Forward with understanding!' As for me, I see nothing to be understanding about." I spoke with finality.

"VC, my man. Look how late it is. Wouldn't it be better if we stopped arguing and you just let me get on with it?"

"Sekuru Saba, what you want simply won't work. Don't you have a home, a partner, and a child to look after? I know we smoke weed together but you should still respect me and your family. Respect is a two-way street. So you want me to be cold for the rest of the night because I have given you my bed and blankets? If you were alone we could have shared my bed. You know how small my place is. Let's discuss other issues rather than this one."

Saba did not answer. He dragged on his cigarette in the dark and it glowed brightly. He gave a deep rasping cough and spat toward the wall.

"OK, what if I give you ten bucks?"

He was as relentless as a fly that smelled shit.

"Uncle, if I ask you a favor and you refuse, I never try to force you or bribe you. If you want to book my room, where will I sleep? Besides, you know I don't have a shortage of money."

Sekuru Saba did not answer. He was as silent as a man standing before the crucifix in church. I thought the matter was settled. Then he lost it. In a rage, he smashed the beer bottle that he had been holding, seeing that I was not going to yield to his demands. The bottle exploded like a gunshot. I was stunned before deciding how to act. This did not merely anger me but maddened me. My anger boiled up as though I were a banded cobra whose back had been injured by a farmer's plough during tilling. It was only the advent of a fuming and ranting Mai Jazz that cooled my anger. I was left holding the smoking gun as Sekuru Saba, knowing Mai Jazz's rages, made a quick getaway with his floozy and was swallowed in the darkness. In order to calm things down, I closed my door and made as if to follow Sekuru Saba and his woman. I left Mai Jazz's words ripping up and pounding the night behind me.

I didn't go far; I soon found Sekuru Saba and his tart huddled against each other and canoodling in the hedge next to the tuck shops. I made an immediate about-face, like someone going to bathe in the river when the cattle got there before him and muddied the waters. I wrapped my arms around myself but to little effect. I had left my room with no upper garments on. I only wore a pair of shorts. That's when I realized that it was almost dawn because of the breeze that was giving me goosebumps. The rough road beneath my feet reminded me that I had come out without my flip-flops, all in an effort to get away from Mai Jazz's stinging words. That woman's mouth is the sharp spear that was referred to by Marshall Munhumumwe. I reasoned that the time was ripe for me to sneak back into my room and go to bed as, by now, Mai Jazz should have gone back indoors.

I was walking through the gate of Mai Jazz's house; we just call it a gate because it is the way in and out, though there is no physical gate. It was once there, but it fell down long before I lived at Mai Jazz's. I stepped into a puddle of sewage that I had not noticed. It was disgustingly sticky. The human waste I had stepped in revolted me by sending a foul whiff. Anyway, we had become accustomed to sewage in Chitungwiza. Don't people say that even the blind know that they have arrived in Chitungwiza owing to the smell? I cleaned my foot using the dry sand in the yard, rubbing it vigorously to the point of almost bruising. Many things pass through sewage pipes, poop, fetuses, cotton wool, used condoms, snot, and vomit. Ugh! It's really nauseating! I only stopped rubbing my foot when startled by a noise that came from a place clothed in darkness behind the hedge. As someone who is afraid of witches, I was glad to discover it was only dogs, including Harare. They were biting each other and growling, fighting for a bitch that was running away from them. I hurried indoors as my nose had started streaming from the cold. I tried to clench my teeth and sniff the snot back where it came from, but without much success. Quietly I chuckled at my phobia that had made me think the pack of dogs were some scary things of the night. Looking forward to continuing my interrupted sleep while my blankets were still hopefully warm, I realized that my bladder was full. It seemed like a good idea to go and empty it before retiring. The toilet at Mai Jazz's house was outside.

There were sounds of heavy breathing and struggling coming from the toilet. I stopped, my heart thumping. I was terrified, thinking that I was about to be beaten up by the goblins or witching-birds of mythic fame. Restraining the urge to scream, I stood stock-still and miserable like a child that has messed its pants when it is old enough to ask for the toilet. I was so frightened that the cold I had been feeling left me and I began to sweat. Then there came a muffled whimper, which floored me with fear. Then came a whisper in a voice that I recognized. That brought me back to my senses. I neared the door to investigate what the whispering was all about at that hour. I thought maybe she was helping someone who had been taken sick. Trembling a bit, I opened the toilet door. I discovered Saru bent over in front of Heaven's husband Eddie, the way one does when planting root crops, her dress lifted high. The man's trousers were around his knees. They both looked at me as one does when discovered behind a bush answering the call of nature. Saru could only gasp, "Ah!" like someone who suddenly remembers that she did not lock the door back in Chitungwiza, when she is as far away as Harare.

I simply turned around and went to pee in the hedge behind the house. Forgetting the beer bottle that Sekuru Saba had broken in front of my room, I stepped on it and cut my big toe. It was very painful and the toe bled like a slaughtered chicken. I limped into my room and tied a dishcloth around it to stop the blood. Afterward I put three pairs of socks on the wounded foot to stop any blood from soiling my bedclothes. I went out to look for a broom in front of Mai Jazz's house. Never being much of a sweeper, I did not own a broom. I found a stumpy one and limped back to my room. The bleeding had stopped, but the toe was itching. I swept the glass fragments together and threw them into the bin. The bin had been knocked over by dogs and they had scattered its contents all over, so I had to put this right first. Afterward I only wanted to sleep. My mind was full of questions concerning Saru and Eddie. The situation was awkward; Saru was a maid, while Eddie was a son-in-law who was staying at his mother-in-law's home. I fell asleep mulling over this issue in my mind. Could it be true? Just what goes on in Harare? Is it an aberration or is there perhaps some issue that needs to be fixed using the traditional cleansing rituals? Truly I don't know. Harare barked outside and I thought he must be through with the other dogs. Harare had no problems like us—me, Sekuru Saba and his tart, Mai Jazz, Saru and Eddie. Harare and his fellow dogs knew nothing about STDs and AIDS.

I felt sleep burying me in a deep grave.

VC and Joyi

Vincent lay on his back in his little one roomer, inspecting its roof in the dimness, which showed that it was daybreak outside. He studied the streaky patterns on the asbestos roof of water from the tiny holes through which light from outside gleamed here and there. The streaks were yellowish like the juice of cowpeas or the piss of drunks on the beer hall walls. If only he could copy these streaks onto a piece of cloth, he would be able to sell it to tourists for a lot of money, claiming that it was the cream of Zimbabwean art. All that would be needed was to label it "Searching for the Spirit" or any other intangible concept—then call it abstract art. He was always talking to his friend about this abstract art. Vincent's main argument was that modern artists hide behind the abstract label when they aren't really producing anything sensible. And when this argument started, it was endless.

Vincent gave a sigh of trepidation. The roof of his little room was so low that really tall people like his brother Bunny could not stand up straight in there without hitting it. Vincent, however, could stand up straight and there was some space between his head and the roof, albeit a small one. Lying on his back, he blinked and felt sleep wrestling with his eyes to close them again. It's a delicious feeling to be able to sleep late, especially when you have a hangover and are feeling languorous. It's an odd sensation. At such times even scratching an itch becomes difficult as the spirit may be willing but the flesh unable.

Vincent was half asleep. He could hear sounds from outside as though from afar but was conscious that they were not part of a dream. He tried to get up, but it was as if he were tied down and had a very heavy person sitting on him. The little strength that he had was fading away as if he were sinking into a murky pool, with water thick as cooked cow's foot jelly. Drenched in sweat, he felt his heart beat fit to dislocate from its usual position and end up in his stomach. Sinking deeper into the slimy water, the stringy algae suddenly transformed into multiheaded snakes.

Some snakes licked him without biting, while others wrapped themselves around his neck. Every time a snake licked him, he became more drained of strength. He tried to open his mouth to scream, but it was shut tight. It did not seem like his own mouth. In an effort to remove the snakes he tried to raise his arms, only to discover that he no longer had any hands.

Eventually, Vincent opened his mouth, but his voice would not come. His tongue protruded like a snake emerging from a cave. As he saw glowing owl-like eyes coming toward him, he heard Harare bark outside, not in anger but in joyous celebration of a new day. He came awake with a start.

Vincent felt his neck with a shaky hand, searching for the snakes around it. He felt sweaty and sat up, raising his head as though it were heavy, but he could see nothing because of the murkiness in his room. His eyes were sticky with sleep. He realized that he had not slept for very long since gazing at the rain streaks on his roof. Feeling shaky, like someone who is narrowly missed by a car when crossing a busy road, he yawned and stretched, expanding his bony chest with its sparse hairs. When he exhaled he smelt the stench emanating from his mouth. It was the smell of traditional brew and teeth that had not been cleaned for some time. He flopped back onto the bed, clicking his tongue.

Vincent lay with his head in his hands with his eyes closed. He adjusted his woolen hat so that it covered his whole head. He let his other hand drift down into his shorts to scratch his itchy pubic hair. That hand was busy down there for a while, and then it came to rest on his belly.

Whenever Vincent overslept he woke up feeling dyspeptic, as if he had cement in his stomach. It was worse when he had drunk masese. He slowly caressed his abdomen, with the languid motions of someone with a hangover. The nightmare from which he had just awakened made it worse. He turned over and looked at the leftover bread from the previous morning, which lay on his little table next to his bed. It had smelled delicious at the time he bought it but now it looked dry. The aroma in the room was no longer that of fresh bread but rather the stench of stale masese, overlaid by stale sweat and unwashed shoes and socks.

The rough homemade knife with a serrated edge like that of a wood saw lay on the table. He had bought it from the Mapostori in Unit H. It was used as a bread knife and had smears of margarine that had become discolored from exposure. More importantly, the knife was used in cutting the cobs of dagga in which he dealt. Corn shucks used in wrapping up the prepared dagga were scattered around and dagga seeds were all over the table and on the threadbare mat.

Vincent rolled over again, smacking his lips as though he were eating something sticky. His movement caused the mattress to squeak and he suddenly started as he realized that he lay in bed with Joyi. He decided to hide his consternation by turning to the wall on which was a banner emblazoned with Bob Marley's image. The banner had the Rasta colors—red, green, yellow, and black—with "FREEDOM" printed at the bottom. He stared at the image and forgot about Joyi's hot breath on him. He read the word "freedom" and smiled, caressing his scraggly beard. Coming back to himself, he tried to remember how Joyi had ended up sleeping in his room.

He could not remember much about what had happened the day before, except that Flabba had come to take him to Makoni in a taxi. After spending the day drinking Chibuku, he had continued his drinking with Flabba, mixing Bohlingers, High Booths, and Viceroy with dagga and braaied meat. Flabba was rolling in it that night. He had a stack of brand-new twenty-dollar notes. Vincent had never bothered to ask where Flabba had gotten the money. He knew that, with the boys, one never asked where they had gotten their money but rather waited to hear them explain for themselves. Besides, if you asked too many questions when your buddy was buying the drinks, he could take it to mean you had had enough and tomorrow you wouldn't want him to treat you well. The last thing he remembered was leaving Makoni for Chinomona Night Club in Unit D. After that he remembered nothing, not even where or how he and Joyi had met.

When he saw the cigarette in Bob Marley's mouth he craved a long joint, long as a wrapper worn by a bride on her traditional wedding day. He turned over and groped under his bed for a packet of cigarettes. He edged closer to the side of the bed so that he could use his whole arm in a sweeping motion. As he moved his arm he struck a glass of water, which fell and broke, spilling water underneath the bed. He clicked his tongue and got up to see what had happened. He was not worried about the glass and stretched out a shaky hand to grab the sodden pack of Madison cigarettes. Fortunately, the cigarettes were not wet. He smiled, took out a cigarette, and put it in his mouth, but quickly removed it. He spat a few times to expel whatever tasted sour in his mouth before wiping it with the back of his hand. Who knows what he had tasted? He put the cigarette back in his mouth and stretched for the box of matches on the table. He ignored the breadcrumbs and dagga seeds stuck to his hand as he lifted the matchbox and went ahead with lighting his cigarette.

When he struck the match, it lit up his face. He had a dark complexion and could have been considered good-looking if only he had better grooming. Long dreadlocks stuck out from under his black woolen hat. Vincent frowned as if in distaste at the smoke belching from his cigarette like a coal steamer. The smoke rose up the room in lazy spirals. He took two quick drags and lay still, savoring how the smoke tickled his lungs, then let it out through his nose.

"If she does not give me my money, she will see. I don't rely on witchcraft but I myself am . . . Haa, voetsek Harare!" Vincent heard his landlady, Mai Jazz, pass by his door, grumbling.

Yeah, she's at it so early in the morning. This mama can really shout. At least I have already given her rent, in fact she owes me thirty dollars, Vincent said to himself, dragging on his cigarette.

As Joyi was snoring away there was a knock on Vincent's door. He did not bother to get up. He answered from where he lay, "Ha, who's there? I'm not up yet." He chucked the stub of his cigarette into the spilt water beside his bed. It sizzled as it went out.

"Ha, VC, my man, open up, I've brought you some good trade."

He recognized the voice at once and smiled a little. "But Sanchez, why do you love to wake me up so early? Man, you always wake me up when—" The voice outside did not allow him to finish his sentence.

"My man, get up and fix me up chop chop. I'll be late for work. You know very well that some of us can only work when high," Sanchez said hurriedly.

Vincent, or VC as his friends called him, opened his door, which screeched from lack of oil. He squinted against the sun's sudden brightness in his face and rubbed his eyes.

"What's up, my man?" Sanchez asked, sidling closer to VC's door.

"Nothing much. Can't you see I'm just getting up?"

"Ah, that's all good. You are one of the indigenous businessmen that Bob and his government are talking about. You must get up late now and then to show that the wealth is now in the hands of us blacks," Sanchez said, laughing, showing his stained teeth, of which the two front ones were missing.

"Right, what can I do for you?" Vincent asked, reaching his hand out for the money. He had no shirt on, just the very crumpled green shorts that he had slept in.

"Make it ten sticks, my man, and also take for yesterday's two sticks," Sanchez stuttered.

Vincent looked at the money that he had been handed and smiled. He did not want to talk much, fearing that Sanchez might just say, "On second thought, make it only three." He rushed into his room and moved things around, grunting as if lifting something.

"Ah, Sanchez man, you've raised me up high. Now, as you know, my shop specializes in good grade, the best from Malawi." He was now gushing in gladness that his day had started off with good business.

"I'll see you at the weekend, my man, when I come for my cassettes. Seems you want to do your marketing and advertising on me. I'll be late for work, and that will mean no more bucks for weed!"

Sanchez put his sticks away in his little bag. He rushed out to his kombi, which he had left parked and idling on the road, and took off with such a leap that VC could only shake his head, eyes sparkling with the pleasure of holding money.

VC did not hang around outside, as the morning breeze felt chilly against his bare skin. He was also scared of Mai Jazz—if she saw him with so much money, she would probably pester him to lend her some. If she paid back her debts willingly it would not be so bad, but one had to chase her and chase her.

The young man gave a start as he entered his room as he had forgotten that Joyi was still there. He feared for the money he was holding as she might influence him to squander it all and he'd be left without any capital. Joyi would never steal it, as he had beaten her almost to death the previous year. When he had heard his landlady threatening eviction or the police, he stopped beating the girl and asked Mai Jazz to understand how Joyi had wronged him. Mai Jazz's house was good for doing business and all his customers knew where to find him so he did not want to move.

Mai Jazz was just threatening; she would never evict VC because he fixed lots of things for her and helped her in many small ways. VC could pay rent three months in advance or buy her meat when she had gone for days eating vegetables from her garden. VC knew how to get on with his landlady. Even though Mai Jazz treated him as a lodger, he was slightly different from the other tenants. He had been there the longest—the Senior Lodger. They knew each other well. VC knew that Mai Jazz could never let a day pass without shouting about something, this was just another of her characteristics, like her nose or her ears.

VC repositioned the mealie meal tin under which he kept his dagga stocks and wiped his hands on his shorts. Sniffing back thin mucus and clenching his teeth, he picked up the milk bottle, which he used as his water bottle, and held it to his lips while looking up, and swallowed. His Adam's apple bobbed up and down like a float on a fishing rod. Some of the water trickled down his chin, flowing through his sparse beard, which was covered in fluff from his blanket. He sighed and then burped, his bulging eyes red as a stop traffic light. As he scratched his butt with his hand inside his shorts, he turned to face the sleeping Joyi.

"Hey, Joyi." Silence.

"Hey, Jo-o-o-y-y-y!" His voice was now raised.

"Ummmm-m," Joyi responded.

"Hey, get up, don't just go 'Ummm' as if you were in your p-p-pa's f-f-ive-star hotel." VC was now stammering, unsmiling. His anger could always be detected by his stammering. "G-g-get up and go home."

"Mmmm-mmm, please let me sleep a bit longer, VC shaz," she said, snuggling into a filthy blue blanket.

"Don't be a pain. I want to do my stuff." He snatched the blanket away. The girl was left bare-skinned except for her bra and black pants stitched along the sides with red thread. Maybe it was to adjust them to make them fit, who knows?

"VC, sha, do I ever mess you around? If you are doing something I could even help." She said this wrapping her arms around herself, not from modesty but for warmth.

"You think no one knows you are always looking for a place to stay? You don't fool anyone here. If you spend the day here you will want to wash with my towel and my soap, in water that I pay for. After that you will want tea with sugar and eggs, then sadza in the afternoon and evening, with meat. Then tomorrow you'll do it again, and eventually you'll say you are going to fetch your clothes and we'll end up living together. It doesn't work Joyi, it just doesn't. You'll be pulling my business back. You know my business: no wife, no kids, no relative, and no—"

"Ah, how can you say that? Did we break up, VC, my darling? Don't I treat you well?" she said in a wheedling voice, rubbing her hands to take away the coldness after the blanket had been snatched away.

"And how often do you treat me well? Isn't that only when you have nowhere to stay? Do you think I haven't heard that your brother threw you out? Weren't you thrown out because you had spent two months staying with Teki in Unit C and only left there after his sisters ganged up to beat you? I'm no fool," VC attacked, lighting another Madison, which seemed to point at Joyi in warning.

"Sha, I told you that my brother Silas is a real dog, just like Harare. Since he married that little wife of his who thinks that talking English and changing her clothes many, many times—"

"Joyi, what you're saying is rubbish. Do you realize that when you left here in December last year that was the last we saw of each other? If it wasn't for the fact that yesterday I was at Chinomona looking for my buddies, you wouldn't be here now." VC exhaled smoke, curling his lips like a spoon.

"Oh VC, if only you knew that I was looking for you. If I hadn't found you then I would have been waiting here for you. Why, it was me who helped you home." She sat up with a pillow over her breasts, which bulged over the top of her dirty bra.

"Joyi, do you know that when you left here the last time, I was raided by the police?" he said, knocking ash from his cigarette into a cup that contained dried tea leaves.

"VC, you might think—"

"There's nothing to think about. I was told by my police pals that it was you who sold me out." The cigarette dipped up and down with his speech.

He threw her clothes at her and told her to dress.

"OK, just let me tidy this place up a bit for you before I leave."

"What do you see here that needs tidying?" VC snarled.

Unfazed, Joyi replied, "Sha, can't you see all this mess?"

Now in a foul mood, VC cried, "Hey, is it your mess or mine?"

Joyi said nothing, she just sighed, holding her clothes gingerly as if they were raw meat. The silence was like in church at prayer time.

—

"Hey Saru, why are you such a trial? You want to scour my pot using sand? I'll make you buy a new one, do you hear me? Not even five months of your pay is enough to buy a new one, do you hear? Are you mad?" Mai Jazz was onto a new issue outside. She could never spend a day without scolding her maid at least ten times. Throughout the day it would be "Saru, what's the matter with you?," "Saru, are you crazy?" Saru this and Saru that . . . Saru kept her silence as though she had neither mouth nor heart to feel any pain from her employer's words.

Vincent was thrilled, thinking of the money he now had. For the past two weeks he had been trying to get some decent money. His mind flashed back to the argument that he had had with his elder brother, Bunny.

"Young man, if you're finding it hard to live in Harare, go home and help the old folks with their farming, do you hear," Bunny said, looking annoyed. Vincent had spent some time trying to convince his brother to lend him money.

"But Mukoma Bunny, it's better for me to run my own business than to trouble the old folks in the village," VC said, lighting a cigarette.

"My bro, if only your business were a straight one, without police and adrenaline, I would understand. A business of selling dagga! If you were in a business whose profits we could see, I would understand. Instead, you always want to borrow money to cover the gaps; we never see the profit, so what type of business is it? What will you do without any proceeds?" Bunny asked furiously.

"Blaz, don't be so difficult about it. All I need is for you to lend me money so that I can go to Malawi to buy my stuff. I know you have the money but simply don't want to give any to me. You are selfish." VC spoke with flecks of foam at the corners of his mouth. When it came to argument he was gifted. He could talk without giving the other person a chance to even cough.

"Now listen here, young brother. I don't want you to come talk to me after smoking your dagga. Was it you who gave me this money you speak of and don't work for? Surely the day you want to marry is the one I will assist or lend you money? Why even—"

"Blaz Bunny, go try preaching at one of the mushrooming Pentecostal churches because your talk is about to make me madder than Malawian dagga," VC said, exhaling smoke.

"Young brother, do something useful. You have nine O-levels, so what's the problem? I even got you a job at my work and you refused it, so what do you really want?"

"Blaz, thanks very much for the job offer, but I can't work for a mere $1,200 a month. I can make that or more in a day."

"You'll wake up the day you are arrested, young man."

"I'll only be arrested when all the cops from here, who are my weed customers, are all transferred to Mutorashanga or Beitbridge, blaz." He blew out smoke and winked.

Bunny left in a huff, got into his car, and drove away to his lodgings in Zengeza.

—

"Vincent, I'm off. Are you deaf now?" Joyi spoke from the doorway, clutching her handbag. "Penny for your thoughts?"

"When did you become the police wanting to know my thoughts? If you really want to know what I am thinking, pass through Unit H and ask the prophet who is there twenty-four hours a day, seven days a week. After all, it's on your way."

"Ah, VC sha, let me go, it seems you don't want to see me."

"So you sleep at the houses of all the people you see?"

Joyi said nothing and left, realizing that VC was in a foul mood.

"These whores are a problem. They are real bitches riddled with AIDS," he muttered to himself.

Harare, Mai Jazz's dog, poked his head into VC's room and wagged his tail so hard his body shook.

"Yes, Harare, what do you want, my friend?"

Harare answered by whining to show he wanted something. VC took bread from the table and felt that it was brick hard. He threw it to Harare, who caught it in midair and went away with it.

VC shut his door and sat on the bed to count his money. He took out more money hidden in the battery compartment of his radio and counted it together with the other money. "One thousand and four hundred bucks. Not bad for a start."

There came a knock at his door. Tucking the money into his woolen hat, he shouted, "Come in!"

Zengeza 3, Mpini Drive

"Mukoma Bunny, ma'am says come and watch the drama on TV."

"Which drama is it?"

"It's called *Madhiri MuHarare* and it's very entertaining. It started last week."

"Ah, if it started last week then I won't be able to follow it because I won't know what happened previously. I don't enjoy dramas much. I find them hard to follow. I prefer the news. Maybe they'll show the highlights from yesterday's soccer match between CAPS and Dynamos, and that I can watch."

"So, what shall I say? Are you coming?" The maid was patient with me.

"I have not cooked yet so I'll do that first. If I finish early I'll come. I may be late because washing dishes is hard for me. It usually takes me a long time."

"OK, Mukoma Bunny. But, if you like, I can wash your dishes for you, I can even do your laundry and ironing as well."

Bunny laughed to himself at the manner of his landlady's maid. The way she talked enticingly as though she were propositioning him. As bothersome as a goat's head that must be cooked with its horns!

Bunny was still thinking about starting to cook. His problem was not only figuring out what to cook, but all the plates and pots that he had used the previous day were still sitting in a bowl unwashed. He started to undo his tie while saying to himself, *Why bother? Get in your car and buy something from any of those little restaurants and takeaways at Chikwanha.* Bunny generally found food from these types of shops disgusting, so another thought was, *Just cut some bread and make a sandwich with the canned beef you bought yesterday.* Still thinking about his meal, he left the kitchen-cum–sitting room and went into the bedroom, where he put his tie and watch on the bedside table before flinging himself onto the bed he had left unmade when he went to work that morning.

So what have I decided to eat? he asked himself, scratching his cheek. As he lay considering what to eat, he heard footsteps coming toward his room. He didn't get up, and the door suddenly opened without anyone knocking.

"Bunny, why are you being so uncool? I told Saru to call you to watch the television. Is there anything wrong? Are you shy?"

"I'm not shy. I just wanted to cook. I'm famished."

"Ah, we cooked plenty of sadza so you can come and join us. We can all eat together while watching the drama, then afterward you can watch the news. I heard you like the news."

"I thought . . . maybe . . . when I've . . ."

"Bunny, why act so rural when you are in town? What you are doing here is done by the Eversmiles and Mativavariras when they have been bought a Fanta at the growth point. How can someone refuse sadza when they are hungry? I think you want further persuasion before reluctantly agreeing as if there were no choice. By the way, where did you say you grew up, Bunny?" Maud asked, one hand on the door, displaying a shaven armpit.

"I was born kumusha, that is where my mother and father are, and I grew up there herding cattle. But I came to Harare to begin school. So I suppose I could say I grew up in Harare because I never went back kumusha except for the school holidays." Bunny was now seated on the bed facing Maud.

"Exactly where did you live? Harare is big, isn't it?" Maud just wanted to keep him talking. Bunny thought to himself, *I don't know what's wrong with some people, they don't seem to have the gift of discerning whether they are bothering someone or not.* Maud was annoying Bunny with her reams of questions. If he had been his younger brother VC, he would have told her that she was pestering him, but Bunny, being Bunny, persevered with answering her questions.

"I lived with my uncle in Western Triangle in Highfields. I only left last year to go and live in a flat in Glen Norah."

"Oh, so you are a Fiyo boy. But Fiyo boys are jacked up. You surprise me because you behave like a priest addressing a group of mothers' union ladies. Do you drink beer?"

"Not always. My work does not permit me to go with a head aching from a hangover," Bunny replied coolly.

"Didn't you tell me that you are an auditor?"

"Yes, I am an auditor. I think you saw it on my payslip." Bunny was annoyed, but tried to restrain himself.

"Being an auditor is not hard. Isn't it all about arriving at a firm looking grim, making the junior staff run around looking for files then grilling them with questions?" she said, as if this were also her profession.

"But you need to know what is in the files and the direction of the questioning," Bunny replied, undoing his shoelaces.

"Anyway Bunny, let's go eat. You are a Fiyo guy and have no need to act scared or shy of me." She started to walk out, then stopped. "Do I scare you, Bunny?" she asked, looking him straight in the eye.

"No," answered Bunny, like a little boy. His body was beginning to heat up. He didn't like this woman's manner and, besides, women made him nervous.

"Do I make you feel shy?" she went on, not realizing what a hard time she was giving him. Or if she realized it, she was enjoying it.

"A little," he answered, looking down at his feet as he put on flip-flops.

"Is it because I look straight into your eyes?" she said, coming nearer to him. His heart skipped a beat when he smelt her perfume. It was the real thing, not those dilute liquids from the flea markets.

"I think so," he said, at a loss.

"How old are you, Bunny?" she asked, smiling.

"Twenty-eight."

"Why, you are a youngster, just two years younger than me."

Bunny was surprised. She was so well groomed you would swear she was a girl of no more than twenty-five.

"Eh-h-h, what did you say the drama is called?" Bunny said, wanting Maud to get away from him.

"Ugh, Bunny, stop acting like a kid. Am I so old? Didn't I tell you that I want to be called Maud?"

"And what would people say?" Bunny was starting to sweat a little. He realized that this woman was difficult to evade once she had you in her net. His throat ached for just a little beer. Maybe it would give him the strength to answer her.

"That's precisely where people get it wrong," said Maud, getting into lecture mode. "You waste time wanting to know what people think of your life and the way you do things. These are people just like you, and if you try to please them, you'll never have any happiness. Try pleasing all people and tell me how far you get. One will tell you to cut your hair because it no longer looks good, and then another will come and ask why you cut your hair as it was just fine as it was. What do you know about people, B? Open your eyes, Bunny, people don't matter. We all breathe, eat, and go to the toilet, so what makes you listen to another person?"

This woman gushed with the sliminess of okra soup when she spoke.

Mai Jazz

"VC, who urinated on the toilet seat?" Mai Jazz asked, standing with both hands on her waist. She used his nickname, as it was more popular than his real name. VC was sealing envelopes with dagga in them, sitting in his doorway.

"I've just woken up so I—"

"I don't want problems. See that you clean it up." VC was surprised and wondered what this was all about. Having just got up, he had not been to the toilet. Anyway, that is what she would do if her son-in-law did something wrong. She would never scold him because she loved him and was scared that her daughter Heaven would shout at her, so she would just find someone else to blame. It could be VC, another of the lodgers, or Saru. Heaven once had an altercation with her mother in the yard that drew crowds. She had said, "Mother, zip your mouth or I'll hit you. I've done it before and I can do it again right now." Mai Jazz went inside, shouting at the spectators, "Go to your homes. You shameless creatures, must you goggle whenever people are having words?" People laughed and started for their homes, as the spectacle was over.

Heaven is spoiled like a white man's dog that eats from the same plate as its master. In fact, she is more like a dog that wants to wear shoes, forgetting that it is a dog. What is to be done if the master failed to tell it that it is a dog in the first place? Harare is full of marvels.

Landlady

Three months had passed since I started staying with Maud, her son Reuben, the maid, and Maud's younger sister, Charity, who attended a college in the city. One day I drove straight home after work. Drinking beer with the boys was far from my mind. I did not give a lift to any hitchhikers because I was in a lousy mood. I planned to buy two pints of beer when I got to Chikwanha, then go straight home to drink them. Some days are like that, you don't feel like talking, and resting in solitude at home is best.

I was listening to my new Oliver Mtukudzi album. That guy speaks truth to power. He sang, "Today's young men are show-offs . . ." Is he lying? We, today's youth, are destroyed by our misplaced overconfidence. The cars that most of us drive all over the show are either company cars like mine or else they are inherited from dead fathers. See now what we do with the cars. One day someone might buy $800 worth of petrol. All this to go where? Nowhere. Simply drifting through the land looking for beer and chicks. Now, these days, you'll go to the grave early because of these chicks. People are kicking the bucket like nobody's business. It's frightening to think who will be left after the HIV pandemic. This is another reason why I am delaying getting married. How can you tell that someone is OK and does not have the virus?

I did not notice how I got home, as I was lost in thought and talking to myself. I had even forgotten about Tuku's music.

I parked the car, went straight to my bedroom, and relaxed on my bed reading those stories in *The Herald* that I had missed earlier. I was startled when someone knocked on the door and just came in without waiting for a response. I hate it when people do that. That is one thing I dislike—the landlady coming into my room without my go ahead just because she owns the house. That's not right. What if she found me naked?

I did not show her that I was annoyed and that I felt she was unduly familiar with me. I gave her a plastic smile.

"Sorry, Bunny, to disturb you when you are reading your paper."

"No problem. I'm not really reading, I was just scanning the paper looking for what to watch on TV." I had bought myself a small TV, realizing that constantly watching TV with the landlady might compromise me.

"Hey, are all those books on the bookshelf yours?"

"Yeah, they are mine."

"Are you some professor who does not want it known he is a professor?"

"Ah, not at all, it's just that I enjoy reading, so whenever I see a book that interests me, I like to buy it," I said, looking at the books on the shelf.

"I will come and borrow some good novels one of these days. Right now, I've come for something else. Do you mind if I sit down?" I was surprised by her show of good manners and the way she appeared to respect me.

"Sorry, I neglected to offer you a seat," I lied. I did not want her to stay. My bedroom had not been tidied and swept properly in two weeks and I do not like uninvited guests. My underpants were visible where I had hung them to dry. A pair of them was really worn down in the middle. It was quite in contrast to the smart suits I wore. If only I had known, I would have sat in the kitchen. Only, I wanted to relax on my bed while reading.

"My, my, manners, Bunny. How can you forget to offer someone a seat? Well, anyway, it is my fault, as I came unexpectedly. I should have sent the maid to tell you that I wanted to see you. It's only that I didn't want you to come to my place since I wanted to see you in private."

What does this woman mean when she says in private? I thought to myself looking at the glossy lipstick on her thick lips.

"Is all well?" I asked, since she remained silent.

"Bunny, you are so funny. You talk, or rather I should say ask, like an elderly person. When you visit them they ask, 'Is all well?' You tell them all is well and they ask you again in no time at all whether all is well."

"That's right, you might neglect to ask so that the visitor forgets that they have an important message that must be said at once," I said, looking at her. She was wearing a long black dress that reached to her feet but had a slit that started at her thigh. I only noticed the slit when she sat down.

"Yes, it happens, but what I have to say is nothing that will scare you or that I would forget. Are you also studying with the Institute of Chartered Secretaries?" she asked, looking at my books again.

"Yeah. These are just attempts to be noticed at work." I tried to get my mind off her thigh, peeking from the slit in her dress.

"Oh yes, that's what it's all about. So are you almost finished?" she asked, looking me straight in the eye. That was one of her habits. Looking me straight in the eye. I don't know what her eyes did to me. They were soft like a puppy's eyes, eyes that could wash you away like a torrent, against your will.

"I have two subjects left at Part D. Are you also doing CIS?" I said, sighing.

"It was my husband who wanted me to do it, but I'm lazy when it comes to books so I dropped it. Back in those days I worked for Lever Brothers," she said, smiling at me.

"So why did you leave Lever Brothers? It seems to me a very good company." I asked, surprised that she had once gone to work and wondered why she had quit.

"We got new bosses who began to change everything and retrench people, and I was one of those affected. Since then I have tried to get another job but there are just too many university graduates coming into the market, so I finally gave up."

I had never really studied Maud since we had never sat down together. She had a short haircut, as you see in trendy young women who are often found on First Street or at Chicken Inn or Nando's, where you can eat fancy food. Slim girls with hair in cornrows or short hairstyles like men. The hairstyle suited her well as she was only thirty and still looked like a young girl. She was well groomed and her skin was testament to this. She wore no makeup with just lip gloss, which showed off her natural beauty. One thing I disliked about Maud was her smile. There's a certain type of smile that is disturbing to male hearts. This type of smile is not easy, one has to be well practiced, but with Maud it appeared natural. She had such a smile that, if you were drunk, you'd get up and dance. I think she knew that she possessed such a weapon. I gazed at her smiling as she sat on a stool at the foot of my bed. She was fidgeting with her fingers as though she had an itch and I noticed her wedding ring still on her finger. I had never spotted that before. It was not my business after all.

"Bunny, I have a problem and hope you can help me," she said, head bowed as if in prayer. She brought her head up and looked searchingly at me, with eyes that talk.

"I have a problem that requires money. I don't know if you want to hear about it or maybe you can help me without me explaining about the problem?" she said, crossing her legs and leaving her thighs bare. My heart skipped a beat. I felt hot under the collar. She had touched me without physically doing so. I don't like being told trivial stories. I did not want to hear other people's problems. I was in such a bad mood that I did not want to talk at all. Let her, as the landlady, say what she wanted. If someone wants to borrow money, they should just say so, rather than launching into a spiel about how their so and so, who is sister-in-law to their aunty in Chinogwenya across the Mutorahuku River behind the little hill called Muridzowenyoka and married to so-and-so, has done such and such. That is not important.

"There's no need for you to tell me the story. If I have the money I will assist," I said, looking away from her legs.

"But I need a rather large sum, you see. That's the problem," she went on, covering her thighs with her hands, and making me feel slightly embarrassed.

"How much do you need?"

"I don't know if you can manage $3,000?" she said, wanting to see if I would be shocked.

"When do you need it?" I asked.

"As early as tomorrow. Once things work out, I will pay you back." She was no longer smiling.

"OK, I'll bring it tomorrow," I said, thinking there goes the money I was saving to buy a piece of land to build a house on. I consoled myself by thinking that it would be returned since I was not giving the money away.

After that she talked of many things. She told me about her brother who was said to be mad. Then she told me about her older sister who lived in Unit D. She told me about her desire to find someone willing to marry her, not for money or her house, but for love, someone who would be able to love her son Reuben. We talked, or rather she talked, until my bad mood dissolved. She asked me about my girlfriend, about my family, and about work. I was feeling relaxed and warmed to her because she had told me so much. We were surprised when we discovered it was one o'clock in the morning. "Let me go and sleep, Bunny. See you tomorrow."

She got up and so did I. She looked at me and said, "Thank you, Bunny, for the money you have promised to lend me."

"I'm happy to help."

She gazed at me, then gave one of her mind-numbing smiles. "Give me a hug, Bunny. I feel happy that I now have someone to share my problems with."

She moved toward me and we hugged like modern people do in town. Up to this day I don't know who started kissing the other, but that is how it happened. She did not sleep in her room that night.

What happened after that can only be described by those who write romance novels like Harold Robbins. I don't know if it was love, weakness, or madness. What I do know is that I even considered marrying her.

Heaven

Harare stopped near the door to Mai Jazz's house. Inside, someone was cooking food that smelled so good that he craved it. The dog drooled and whined as if to say, "I beg you, please don't forget me when you eat your food."

"Get away from here, you humanlike dog. I'm sure there's something spiritually wrong with this dog. Look at its eyes. This scares me. Pfutseki Harare! It's spoiled by VC, who lets it into his room and gives it titbits. Pfutseki you! Oh look at it, it looks as if it's about to laugh. It will shock us one day when it says, 'You people are very mean.' Don't you think so, Sisi Saru?" Heaven, the daughter of Mai Jazz, was speaking to the maid as she fried chicken, the aroma of which had drawn the dog to the door.

"Heaven, don't scold my dog." Sekuru Hamundigone spoke from outside, patting Harare's head, "Hello Harare, my doggie doggie. What are these people doing to you? This time I won't leave you behind. Don't worry, Harare, all the scolding will come to an end—there's no region without a grave. Who hit my dog on the back causing this gaping wound? What is it? Is it from hot water scalding his back or a disease? You people are cruel." Sekuru Hamundigone spoke while caressing Harare's head. Harare showed his pleasure by wagging his tail vigorously.

"Uncle, how can you talk to the dog before greeting people?" Heaven said, moving toward the door.

"People can speak if they have problems or pain but Harare cannot, so I was just making sure he is OK," Hamundigone said, releasing the dog as he entered the house.

"Where is the sadza? Are you only cooking chicken?" he asked, opening the lid on the pot.

"Uncle, what are you doing? You were touching the dirty dog out there and now you are opening the pot without washing your hands," Heaven shouted.

"Oh, so I am a dog to you?" Hamundigone asked his niece with a glare. Saru cowered in a corner.

"You are no dog, Uncle, but what you did is not hygienic," she replied rudely.

"Hah. Heaven, where did you learn hygiene, when you even failed your mother tongue in form four?" He removed his jacket and walked to the lounge.

"Young man, are you still staying here?" Hamundigone berated Heaven's husband, who was watching TV. Eddie was struck speechless. It was Heaven who saved him. He was terrified because Hamundigone, before he retired, had threatened to beat him up when he last visited.

"Uncle, if you came here drunk, sober up. You want to spoil our happiness. Eddie lives here and you know it. What's your problem?"

"So I'm the fool? I have never heard of an able-bodied young man who has the temerity to live off his mother-in-law. Is that how you behave where you come from? Heaven, you are going too far these days. If you had a father I would have asked him if he received any lobola from this little boy," he said, pointing at her with a dirty finger.

"Uncle, leave Eddie alone. Ask me if there is anything you want to know and I will tell you," she replied, refusing to let Hamundigone harass her man.

"Heaven, it's not my fault you have a loafer for a man. I didn't want to have words with you. You behave like a bad omen," he said, sitting on a tattered sofa.

"Uncle, leave me alone. Take your craziness to the one who cursed you. I'll never fear you no matter what. You want to intimidate people in their own homes. What's your problem?" Heaven blustered like a summer fire.

"Heaven, please answer these questions. Has your man paid lobola? Does your man work? Whose sadza does he eat? Does he pay rent? What is his basis for staying here?" He looked at Eddie, shaking his head in pity.

"Uncle, this is none of your business. This is like trying to converse with airplane passengers when you are a cyclist. What's with this issue of payment of lobola that you are insisting on so much? Are you after the money? Now, when Eddie is ready to pay, I will go and find my father rather than have you, Uncle, take that money. Is that why you let them fire you so that you could come and pester us?" She was now really angry. Saru tried to restrain her and was slapped hard. "Why are you holding me? Are you on his side? I say what I feel like saying. Uncle, this is my mother's house not yours."

Hamundigone glared at Heaven, who looked as if she might climb over him and fly off.

"Heaven, don't start the war songs in my head that had become silent, do you hear me? I fought one war with the enemy; let it be the only one. Why are you trying to start another war? I don't want us not talking in future. You are my niece and I, your uncle, am mad, so I can be ignored, but if I am mad, then you, your mother, and that little man of yours need to be sent to the psychiatric unit at Harare Hospital. Don't think you can bully me; you can't. I fear nothing except fear itself and I'm indomitable. There's nothing new in what you are doing; we have seen it and heard about it before. There's nothing admirable in what you are doing, what you call the Harare way. You found Harare here already. Ah ptu! I don't marvel at a dog's pregnancy as if I can milk it, my niece," he said, leaning back into the sofa whose innards were exposed.

"Uncle, I didn't believe that you were mad, but you have just demonstrated that you are. Go and find your daughter Cleodia and act crazy there instead of bothering us, who are children of others. Also, this war you always talk about has nothing to do with us. I don't even know what Smith, whom you fought, looks like, so don't keep irritating us. Were you forced to go to war?" The matter had now escalated to serious proportions.

Hamundigone heaved a sigh. He wiped off sweat and shook his bowed head.

"Alright, Heaven, let it end because I'm drunk and I'm mad, aren't I? Where is your mother?" Hamundigone asked, getting up. She did not answer.

"She went to the hospital to see Aunt Maud," Saru said, clutching the cheek that Heaven had slapped.

"So how is your aunt? Who sent me the telegram about Maud's sickness?" the teacher asked, bringing out a telegram from his pocket. It was badly crumpled like a burnt piece of plastic.

Heaven did not respond.

"It was sent by her lodger Bunny. She is at the hospital. I have not seen her yet, I just hear reports," Saru answered, after she realized that Heaven was not going to talk to him. Heaven took her man and went to their bedroom and closed the door.

The same thing had happened previously, before Hamundigone became unemployed. They had argued until Heaven threatened to leave with Eddie and stay away until Hamundigone went back to his school. At first they thought she was joking but she meant it, so, in the end, Hamundigone, to solve the problem, went to stay with his other sister Maud in Zengeza 3. That's Heaven, the town girl. Even though her mother was tough, she knew that, when her daughter picked a fight, she was relentless. Mai Jazz was notorious for scolding but, for Heaven, it was both scolding and fighting. When she was still in school and her mother ran a shebeen, she was notorious for fighting with the men who came to drink there. Some women, whose husbands had been beaten up by Heaven, once ganged up on her and she fought them like one possessed until the police had to be called.

When her mother came back from the hospital, she found Hamundigone sitting alone. Heaven and her man did not come out of their bedroom. She did not even come out to ask how her aunt was doing at the hospital. Hamundigone did not sleep there or eat, he refused the food and went to buy a meal at the Chinomona nightclub. He slept at Maud's place. Even though Maud was sick at the hospital, her other sister Charity, younger than Mai Jazz, was staying with Reuben while his mother was at the hospital. Hamundigone would go to the hospital early the next morning.

VC

People like Saba are not good. What kind of person is always thinking of money? When he has it, he will spend it, when he does not have it, he will look for ways of getting it. It does not matter to him how he gets it so long as he gets it. His life is about messing others up. How can he take bread and milk bought by his partner and sell it to get money for dagga? He would even sell the shirt off his back. Now he does not want to repay the money I lent him. He has not paid his rent and his partner and child are starving. I don't think he was born the same way everyone else is. As for his partner, Mai Tanya, one would think he held a gun to her head to make her love him.

University of Zimbabwe

VC arrived at the University of Zimbabwe close to lunchtime. One of the touts at the rank was yelling at those who were trying to jump the queue and get on the kombis as they arrived.

"You people behave no differently from me who doesn't have a degree. I'm better than you. Where are you rushing to? You're going to have the tarts at Terreskane Hotel drink all your money up. Some of you will come back on foot." People in the queue laughed and this encouraged him.

"You're laughing? Do you think I am lying? Come back after two weeks and see. In fact just two days. Some will borrow money from me—me, Kavhukatema. He-e-e-y you. Go back to the queue."

The guy who was trying to jump the queue tried to resist. "No Kavhu, I need to get to the bank before it closes."

"See now, that is how inconsiderate graduates—no, in fact, undergraduates are. Do you think you are the only one rushing for the bank? You . . ." Kavhu, the tout, shouted so that all would hear him.

"Kavhu, I'm not a student," the guy said sneeringly.

"I don't care. Whether you are a professor or the dean of your faculty has nothing to do with me. You've never seen me in your office, but you have come to my office, so you must do what I want lest I embarrass you," he said, moving toward the guy.

The guy realized that he could end up being embarrassed and started for the end of the queue, muttering inaudibly.

"Have you no shame acting like that when you are wearing glasses and a jacket? Hey you. Wait! I need only twelve people to get in there. You over there . . ." he said, hurrying toward a newly arrived kombi that was being mobbed before it had stopped. Those inside could not get out as those outside were pushing, pushing to go to Harare. Yes, Harare was great when you had money, as did these people. Money drove the students crazy; they ended up missing lectures for weeks. They only returned when the money was spent. Some boys needed to be fed at the clinic at the end of last term when they were broke. Those were the university's great drinkers. They even had nicknames based on brand names of beers: there was Mascud and another was Castle the Great. There were so many things happening at the university that were nothing to do with books or anything academic.

It was clear that students had been given their loan payouts by the way the boys were drinking bottled beer. They wandered round the campus singing obscenities, harassing people, and even poured beer on solitary girls as they went past. Some smashed bottles on the ground, then leaped up and down like school children in the playground shouting "Ahoy!" Some had no shirts on, others had no shoes, others had their flies open, and others had their trousers rolled up.

The minibus queue to the city was long. The girls were going to town to buy the latest fashions and cosmetics. Hair treatments would also be sought to transform hair that resembled a neglected lawn. VC was surprised by the number of plastic bags carried by those who had come with him from town. He had not noticed them, as he had boarded the kombi last. Some of the boys had bought ghetto blasters from the Indian shops in Harare. They were headed for their campus residences, where they'd make noise in the corridors.

VC did not spend a lot of time watching the boys, who called themselves the University Bachelors Association. He adjusted his leather cap, with its Rasta badge on the front. It suited him very well. He had bought it in Fiyo, during the days when he procured his dagga from the place in Highfield known as Beira Corridor, before it was raided and closed by the police. It was genuine leather, but the guys he bought it off simply asked for "two reds," meaning two ten-dollar notes.

VC walked away from the kombi rank and passed through Swinton Hall for Girls. It was a well-known shortcut to the UZ community. He left the tout Kavhu to his struggle with recalcitrant commuters. As he was descending the steps into Swinton, VC heard Kavhu say, "You educated people are uncooperative. Hey you, go to the back of the queue or else I'll leave you to push and shove and have the little money that is making you so wild filched."

One boy yelled, "Yes, let us alone, go!"

Who knows what happened next since VC went into Swinton. He was surprised at the buying power these students had, buying power that gave them immense joy. All the faces around him were radiant. In Swinton, he noticed a queue of girls at the payphone. Next to them was a group of smartly dressed boys and girls preaching. There was a young man roaring and lifting his bible in the air. He was preaching in English with hilarious grammatical slips. His verbosity included big words not commonly used in speech. Most of the girls waiting to phone appeared annoyed by his preaching. A young woman with hair extensions inside the phone booth opened the door and poked her head out. She was tall and slim, fair in complexion, and had a ring in her nose. She stretched her giraffe-like neck, frowned, and said, "Excuse me, you are violating my privacy. I have important things to talk about on the phone and I can't hear anything. Could you please move somewhere else?" Hearing her without having seen her, you would think it was a white person complaining.

The preacher took no notice but continued his preaching while the others called out, "Ame-e-e-n. Ame-e-e-e-n."

This annoyed the young woman so much that she slammed the door to the booth so hard that it flapped about. The other girls just clicked their tongues and shook their heads as if they were emerging from an Apostolic baptism. Whether they were annoyed by the girl speaking English, or what she said, or the preaching, or all of the above, or something else is not known. VC did not know and went by in silence.

He came out of Swinton facing the student services center, which had banks, the clinic, a supermarket, and other services. The place was packed as if there were about to be a meeting. Some were walking in groups and laughing and talking, while others were rushing to the banks to cash their checks. Most were coming from the lecture theaters though. Maybe they would get their money the following day. This reminded VC that he had to get to Complex 4, where Magi was, quickly. The girls were mostly talking about the outfits they had seen in town, which they wanted to buy. Suddenly VC saw someone like Magi going into the post office and he turned to follow her. He quickly went down the stairs beside the overcrowded post office and pushed his way through, "Excuse me. Excuse me."

"You, don't push in. We have been here for a long time!" a young man called out.

"Do you think I bank with the post office, which doesn't have any ATMs?" VC asked rudely.

"My friend, don't be rude. We are bored standing in this queue while others are already finishing the beer over there," another young man, wearing glasses like a fly's eyes, replied.

VC did not respond. The person he had mistaken for Magi was not her, so he left. He did not want to continue arguing with the students, as he had heard that the university boys could be uncouth, but he feared missing Magi more than getting into a fight. He was used to dealing with dagga users, which made him a fighter.

As he was leaving he saw a girl who had been at school with him in form four, two years previously.

"Hey, Vincent, you haven't changed," she said, greeting him.

"Hi, Fortunate, what's up?" he replied, shaking her hand and not letting go.

"Nothing. School has started so we are swotting just like school kids do," Fortunate replied, pulling her hand away.

"So you are banking some money? You must have plenty of it," said Vincent, eyeing the money in her hand.

"Not at all. See." Fortunate showed Vincent the registered envelopes she was carrying.

"What are they?" he asked, looking closely at them.

"I'm sending money kumusha, my friend. There are lots of things there that need money. So where did you do your A-levels? Which faculty are you in?" Fortunate said, changing the subject.

"I'm in agriculture and specializing in tobacco," VC said, smiling. He didn't want to stay talking for too long in case he missed Magi. He said his goodbyes to Fortunate, patting her shoulder.

Fortunate was left astonished that there were people who would start specializing in their first year at university. She did not know that VC had been specializing in dagga for many years.

VC arrived at Complex 4 and saw a group of young women sunning themselves and chatting. There is always a smell that lingers in the corridors of the university complexes. The odor struck him in the face. Whether it was perfume or different cosmetics all mixed up, it was hard to tell. With the boys' corridors, on the other hand, it was the odor of beer, unwashed bodies, and dirty clothes—especially shoes worn with unwashed socks.

He knocked hard on the door when he reached Magi's room. What he had feared was about to happen. No one answered.

He knocked again and the girl in the next room came out.

"Are you looking for Magi?" The girl looked as if she had been sleeping, as she was stretching and yawning. Her face was striped from whatever she had used for a pillow.

"Yeah," VC replied, fumbling with his cap.

"I was not here when she left, but you can ask the girl in the third room from this one. Over there," she said, pointing to Kundai's door.

"Alright, thanks." VC walked away and the girl followed behind on her way to the toilet.

VC knocked on Kundai's door and asked where Magi was.

"Magi went to Mbare to get her hair braided. Who are you?" asked the stunningly beautiful, but oh so skinny, girl. Perhaps she had the virus. If there came a strong wind it would probably carry her away.

"Damn it," VC said, slamming his hands together. "I am her brother. Did she leave anything?"

"Her nameless brother, is it?" Kundai smiled, showing a large gap in her teeth that looked almost like a missing tooth.

"My name is VC," he replied, frustrated.

"VC, are you the Vice Chancellor? No, don't take me seriously, I am just kidding. Let me give you what she left for you." She could see that VC was too frustrated to listen to anything else she might want to say. She brought an envelope from her room and handed it to VC. He opened it with slightly trembling hands and counted the money inside.

"Is that all?" he asked, holding $500.

"That's all she gave me," replied Kundai, no longer smiling.

"She was supposed to give me $1,000," VC said, looking badly let down. "Don't you have $500 to make it $1,000? She'll sort you out when she comes back. If I don't get it, I'm in serious trouble, sister."

"It's difficult. If only she was here."

"Sister, please help. If you could lend me just $200 then I can make do. Things are really tight."

Kundai was silent for a while thinking.

"Please sister, I'm begging you. I am a businessman but things are not going my way."

"I might be able to lend you $500 but if Magi refuses to give me my money back, you must pay it. Since you are a businessman, I believe you are honest." She reached for her wallet on the table. "Ah, I had almost forgotten. She said you must pass through Complex 3, second floor, here is the room number she wrote. She said there is a boy who needs some headache medicine." Kundai handed him a piece of paper with a number and name written in red pen.

He took both the money and the paper and put them in his pocket.

"So you treat headaches?" Kundai asked.

"I only treat chivanhu problems, those that stem from spiritual issues," VC said, taking off. He went straight to Complex 3. That is what he liked about Magi, she would get him customers from among the dagga smoking young men at the university. He smiled as he descended the steps from Complex 4 leading to Complex 3.

Kundai, left standing at her door, shook her head, "His manner is just like Magi's. Fancy being so similar."

The Hood

Harare was lying by the fallen gate. His eyes were dark like shillings kept in an old woman's snuffbox. He lifted an ear when he heard the sounds of utensils from the house, immediately leapt up, and ran to the washing up spot, where the plates from the previous night had been placed. He ran with a sideways gait as though crippled and arrived at the same moment that Saru came out of the house carrying a dishrag and a piece of brown soap. She stood by the door looking for something to beat Harare with. When she found nothing she hurled the soap at Harare with such force that it lifted her dress.

"Nxa! Pfutseki, Harare," she yelled, as the soap she had thrown missed the dog and hit a glass, which smashed to smithereens.

She quickly looked around to make sure no one had seen her. There was just Vincent, who was sitting outside rolling a spliff. Saru didn't mind that he had seen her shatter the glass, as he was her buddy who would never sell her out to Mai Jazz.

She called again, "Pfutseki! What's up with this dog?"

Harare merely cocked his head and went on looking for anything that could be chewed or licked—anything to relieve his hunger pangs. Did anyone ever give him food? If he did not find his own, he would starve. That's what it's all about in Harare.

He poked his snout into a glass that still held the remains of a drink and wiped it clean with one sweep of his pink tongue. Next, he nudged a blue bowl with flowers painted on its side; its lid was on but as Harare pushed it, it fell over, spilling chicken bones with no meat left on them.

Saru walked quickly toward Harare. He was a funny-looking black dog with a drunken mouth that appeared to be on the verge of laughter. The scalding wound on his back was almost healed, but there were a few flies plaguing him.

When Saru approached, Harare backed away and stopped near VC.

"You people, leave this dog alone. What's your problem?" VC said, licking the spliff he was rolling to make it stick properly.

"I want to hit him. Look, he broke a glass," said Saru, pointing at the glass she had hit with the soap.

VC did not say anything, he just smiled and lit his spliff. The smoke swirled around the tree in the yard before being carried away on the pure morning breeze.

Saru picked up a stick and hid it behind her back. With the other hand she grabbed a bone from the blue serving bowl. She started moving toward Harare pretending that she wanted to give him the bone. Harare sat on his haunches and watched Saru, head tilted. He cocked one ear and made as if to wag his tail, then stopped abruptly.

As Saru was nearing, VC yelled, "Run Harare, she wants to hit you."

Saru threw the stick, but the dog was well away.

"Harare, I'll get you with your human-like eyes," Saru said, looking at the gap in the hedge that was Harare's escape.

"Hey you, do you think I pay you to spend your time playing with Harare? Have you finished your work? Bwarare! Bwarare!" Mai Jazz emerged from the house putting toothpaste on her toothbrush.

"If you continue messing around you will leave Harare and go back to dusty kumusha. I don't want someone that I pay to annoy me."

VC immediately slipped into his room, the ganja fumes trailing behind him like a shadow.

Mai Jazz was well known as a scold. She could scold endlessly. That is where she got the nickname Mai Jazz. It was said sarcastically that when she started shouting, she sounded like the high-sounding horns in jazz. VC ran to escape being shouted at. Besides, Mai Jazz was not dressed properly. She had on only an old nightie that was so thin from washing that it was virtually a sieve. It left nothing to the imagination. If she had pants or a bra on it might have been better. If she were dark-skinned it might have been less revealing, but she was very light in complexion.

Saru was saved by the fact that Mai Jazz was brushing her teeth. As she tried to shout the toothpaste sprayed out with her words. She became silent as two policemen suddenly appeared on their way to buy some weed from VC.

The Dude

"Sanchez now goes to church and no longer drinks. He has even stopped smoking. That is just not possible? He's my buddy and I know him." VC mumbled deliriously, turning over in his little bed.

"VC, wake up. What are you going on about?" Joyi spoke watching VC, who had been badly battered. His eyes were sunken from the swelling. The bandages in which he was wrapped like homemade cigarette paper made it look worse.

He lifted a hand weakly and said to Joyi, "When they are loaded with money they wash their dishes with Geisha bath soap."

"Who, VC?"

There was no answer.

"VC, how are you doing?" she asked, edging closer to the bed. She sat on a small bedside stool.

"I'm in pain, my dear," he groaned.

"Shall I give you some porridge?"

"Wait, I'll eat later. Right now it is not possible."

"VC love, do you realize you have not eaten since you came back from the hospital yesterday?"

"I'll eat, let me be for now," he coughed, screwing his eyes tight.

"Just get up and eat sha-a, you don't—"

"Is he up yet, Joyi?" Mai Jazz interrupted, coming into the room when she heard them speaking. She had returned from kumusha, where she had gone to bury her younger sister, Maud. When she had arrived earlier in the afternoon, she had found him asleep so had left him to rest.

"Yes, he's awake, but he won't eat," Joyi replied, moving aside to create space for Mai Jazz.

"What have you done, my son VC? How terribly hurt you are," she said. She looked at the young man lying on the bed.

"It doesn't matter, mother," he replied, groaning.

"Joyi, how could they release someone in this state from the hospital? What do they expect us to do?"

"They said there are no beds."

"This won't do at all. Has his brother Bunny come yet? He left the funeral before us."

"Yes, Bunny said he is going to court and will pass through here to pick VC up and take him to his home. But VC is refusing to go because he says it will mess up his business."

"Is he mad? How can he think of business when he is wounded like this? How will he sell and talk in this state?"

"I don't know. I also asked him that. He says he will be OK the day after tomorrow. Maybe you should force him to eat so he can take his pills."

"VC, get up and eat a little, my son."

He didn't answer, just shook his head gently in refusal.

“What do we do if you won’t eat?” Mai Jazz asked in dismay.

They heard a car stopping at her gate.

“Is that not the police, Joyi?”

She got up and peered out of the door, then came back inside. “It’s not the police. Even if it was them, we cleared all that stuff from here. It is Bunny and some woman.”

Magi and Bunny realized that they could not leave VC at his lodgings given his state. Even though he did not want to leave, they lifted him up and left Joyi to wait for contraband that was due to arrive that evening. They helped him limp to the car slowly, Magi looking on the brink of tears. Heaven and Eddie stood sullenly by the wall.

Harare

“Hey! Whose dog is that?” With a piece of meat in butcher’s paper wrappings in his mouth, Harare swiftly leapt over the puddles of sewage on the street and crept into a drainage pipe under a bridge. This is not unusual in Unit D life. Be it theft by dogs or humans, that is the way of it. After all, who is not stealing?

Harare was Mai Jazz’s dog; she had been given him by her white employer when her employer fled the country and returned home to Britain.

“Jerina, do you suppose you can look after this dog or should I take him to the SPCA?”

“Do you think I would fail to look after a dog that I have been feeding all along? I will look after it. I love it a lot.”

The idea that Jerina, or Mai Jazz, loved the dog greatly pleased her white bosses so that their eyes, like discarded coins used for ritual purposes, briefly shone. They knew that Jerina could look after the dog since it was her who shampooed, groomed, and fed him.

“Miriam, I will leave some money for Jerina in the bank so she can buy Salisbury’s food when we are gone. We’ve already paid for two years’ worth of food at the Newlands Pet Shop, haven’t we?” queried the husband.

"Yes, there are two years' worth of food there, all she has to do is fetch it. I have already given Jerina all the papers. It's up to her now. Jerina, I know you people feed your dogs sadza, there's nothing wrong with it, however please don't feed my Salisbury sadza every day. Sorry, I'm repeating myself, but you know where we get the dog's food. We have an account there. It's all there in the papers I gave you. You will get pet food for him, won't you? Is that OK?"

"I hear you, madam."

"Jerina, we really wanted to take Salisbury with us, but we don't know if we will get jobs quickly or where we will be living, so you will have to do everything for him that we used to do. He has a very good pedigree," the husband added.

True, they loved their dog greatly, but Zimbabwe had come unexpectedly and they joined those whites who had already fled to leave the blacks to mess up on their own.

As soon as the whites left, the dog moved to the ghetto in Seke, Unit D. Jerina, a black domestic worker in the suburbs, was lucky enough to get a pension so that she was able to buy a house in Unit D.

Life was alright for the first six months after the whites had left. Jerina squandered the money she had been left to buy food for the dog after closing the Newlands Pet Shop account, saying the dog had been run over by a bus. Even so, Salisbury was still eating well. He was no longer being shampooed though. Who wants to be seen shampooing a dog in the ghetto? That's white people's stuff.

Things started changing as Mai Jazz became accustomed to life in the location. When she was made the political commissar in the Zanu-PF Chimedzamabhunu Women's League Branch, Salisbury's name was changed to go with the times. He became Harare. Mai Jazz began to neglect the dog once owned by her former white employers. She had used the money meant for dog food to buy fridges to start her shebeen. She also managed to buy sofas. In those days money still had buying power.

The dog was very sick during this period; he refused to eat sadza and refused to answer to the name Harare. He no longer played. He was pitiful, like a child who had lost both parents on the same day. Harare spent the whole time beneath the hedge seeming close to death. No one cared. Running a shebeen takes a lot of time and work. Salisbury realized that life had changed and began eating dusty sadza and feeding from bins. He became the Harare we now know. He had arrived in Zimbabwe.

Mai Tanya

Surely, if I die, Saba will be the murderer. How can anyone give his partner an STD with talk of HIV being everywhere? If only I had known, I would have stayed at home with my mother herding goats and growing sweet potatoes. And now Tanyaradzwa is always sick. I have to cope alone. Her misfortune is an uncaring father. Being with Saba was really a mistake, a wrong choice. There was a guy who loved me but I spurned him for this. He disappointed me taking too long to tell me he loved me. He only told me how he felt after I was pregnant by Saba. He really hurt me. He acted crazy, saying he didn't care that I was carrying Saba's baby and that he would marry me anyway. When he had taken so long to declare his love I feared becoming a spinster, and so I plunged into this rubbish pit in which I now find myself. I was also influenced by the conversations I had with my girlfriends. We were all scared of becoming old maids. So now I am cohabiting with him, not married, but in the hopes that he will marry me one day.

I say to him, "It's OK, Saba my love, just give them a little lobola money so that we can be married."

He just clamps his cigarette in his dark lips and drags on it as if it were the very air he lives on. "I never told you to fall pregnant. I did not want to stay with you and I don't want to marry you, so don't bother me with that issue."

"But even if you say you don't love me, give your child a better life." I say this knowing that I am talking to myself.

How can a man bring a whore home? He forced me from the bed so he could sleep there with his whore. I had to sleep on the floor in the same room with my baby in my arms. Everything they were doing was clearly audible to me. I cried so much that I wet the blanket. When he heard me weeping, he got up from his whore and struck me hard with his fists. He beat me up so badly I could not open my eyes or eat for days. When he felt he had hit me enough, or maybe he was just tired, he tore my clothes off and raped me, saying that was what I was crying for so he was giving me my share. If only someone had come to my rescue. But not one person came to save me all the time I was crying, first from the beating, then from the rape. Those who used to intervene did so in the early days, then gave up, saying this was the life I was destined to live with Sabastian. He always hits me so badly that I feel my days on earth are numbered. I have too many internal injuries. When I laugh I feel sharp pains all over and I often take to my bed. I have become an invalid. If I could go back home I would, but I know there's no place for me there anymore. My father would rather be arrested and die in jail for murder than see me. I disappointed him so much that when we meet is the day I die. I don't see why I am punishing myself by staying here. Saba does not come home, does not buy food, and does not love me. I am just waiting for the end of my life. I feel sorry for the baby. Why does life go this way? I don't know.

The Graveyard

I have not been to work for five days. We buried her at her kumusha in Shamva yesterday. It is distressing to hear women wailing when facing the grave's gaping mouth. And the church songs they sang. There is one song that is stuck in my mind and continually repeats. The song goes, "To us is left very little time." It is stopping me drinking or rather I should say getting drunk. I feel devastated and overwhelmed by Maud's death.

For days I have felt trapped, burning tears. Life is a jigsaw puzzle with missing pieces. The way we struggle and labor to build ourselves houses and buy fancy cars that we leave behind when we go back to where we came from. To dust. That is when you see that life is all vanity, as Solomon said in Ecclesiastes. I think I am sick from being overburdened by thoughts about the illness, death, and burial of Maud. Or perhaps I am now mad.

There was a storm in Harare and Chitungwiza violent enough to fell trees and electric pylons. The thunder prevented sleep. I could hear the song "To us is left very little time . . ." in the rhythm of the rain. I am thinking about the young man who got up to preach at the graveside. He astonished us all. He was very young. He said in a loud, angry voice, "If life on earth is this, what is its meaning?" And I think of the words from Mtukudzi's song, "Yesterday we said congratulations when he was born, but today he has been snatched from us." We know we are travelers passing through, but her time was too short. What does it mean, guys? We are tired. We are tired for goodness' sake. We understand when someone old leaves us. But what does life really mean? Is this what we are born for? To be born to fertilize the earth? I think there are other things we should be doing instead of dying young like this. Lead on sister, we will meet in heaven.

Then the young preacher launched into a poem:

Yesterday I honor you,
From you I emerged
Like a chick from the egg.
And about you,
I speak of what I know
That yesterday
We married off Zvipohazvienzani
That it rained in the fields
And that we buried Muzanenhamo.

About you tomorrow
What do I say,
When I have not yet kissed you.
Tomorrow you make me sorrowful.
Will my child ever grow up?
Will we eat, drink, and be merry?
Will there be someone to bury me,
In this walk of the Valley of the Shadow of Death?

He stopped and bowed his head saying, "Let us read from Matthew 27, and Mai Kwaramba will close in prayer."

University of Zimbabwe

Magi's folks would be shocked if they knew that she spends little time in her room because of her lovers. Her mother thinks she is studying while she is busy messing around. Sometimes she comes back in the morning, late for lectures. Sometimes she bunks them because she is tired or she is nursing a hangover. Her boyfriend visits almost every evening. Although I say "boyfriend" he is not a boy. He is a grey-haired man with a wife and grown-up children at home. Magi and her man are forever on the road going to places of entertainment. Yet I think things are better since she got this old man. At the beginning of the year, when she was still going with a fellow student, her roommate would leave the room and stay in the library until closing time. It was impossible for her to study when Magi and her lover were crossing the boundaries of kissing and caressing in her presence. But the other problem then was that Magi was having sex for money. She slept with university guys who paid for her services.

Yet I blame myself for not helping her those times when she came to my room telling her sad story.

"Kundai, my friend, do you know that my boyfriend is a married man?" she told me, painting her nails with my nail polish.

"I-ii Magi, why do you date a married man?" I asked her, astonished at her lack of shame in saying such things.

Though she said "friend," there was no real friendship between us. We were acquainted because we spoke from time to time and stayed on the same corridor. We also did the same courses before I was assigned to an English honors class. Even in the days when we did the same courses, our relationship was based on the fact that she would come and borrow my assignments to copy. How was she going to get time to study when she was madly in love with a medical student? That affair ended because the guy constantly said he was busy. When she importuned him, he told her that it was not good to yoke a horse and a donkey and that it does not do for a doctor to have a relationship with an art student. Imagine how arrogant that was. So that is the way it ended. That is how she became promiscuous.

She sighed before replying, "Shamwari, it's tough. This is my last year in college and I need to get a serious boyfriend before I leave. I am not talking of these guys who just want to sleep with me. I am looking for someone that I can settle down with, not the type that dumps me as soon as I tell them I have a child. They tell me that they don't want someone with an eventful past."

I was shocked. She had never told me that she had a child. "Yes, I do have a child, my friend," she said, seeing my reaction. "She is a three-year-old and I had her by my Shona teacher when I was doing my A-levels. I regret refusing to marry him when he asked. He was a widower with a daughter who was my schoolmate at Mavhuradonha. Her name was Cleodia. I really liked her and we were friends, but the friendship ended when she found out that I had a baby by her father and she hated me. I see her sometimes in Harare. She works at one of the top banks but we don't talk. So this teacher was fined a lot of money by my people for them not to report him. I was pregnant when I wrote my exams. No one knew about it apart from me and Mr. Hamundigone. Cleodia only got to know about it when the baby was born. The baby, Rudo, lives with my mother kumusha, and she simply adores her."

I said nothing. She sighed.

"So, shamwari, I am no longer interested in this married man that I am seeing, but he says that he wants to marry me if I am a good girl. He has a good job at a company in the city. He promised me a job next year so maybe I may just avoid becoming a teacher after I graduate. I hate chalk dust and prattling endlessly to people," she said, frowning as if the chalk dust were already descending on her.

"Magi dear, do you think it is too late to find the teacher who fathered your child? If you say that he loved you, he just may marry you, since you now know what you want from life. It is good for parents to be together so that your child might have a good life." I felt sorry for her. She was wasting herself.

"Shamwari, troubles never end. When I tried to contact him they told me he had been fired. They said he is now mad. It really pained me. I don't think it is possible to marry him anymore."

"What could have caused the madness?"

"I-ii Kundai, I don't know. These war vets are hard to understand," she replied, seeming on the point of tears.

"But the war ended ages ago, I doubt it can be the aftereffects," I said thoughtlessly.

"The war never ended. It morphed into other types and we are right now dodging bullets being fired by poverty and corruption." She said this watching me with her clear eyes, which were embellished with black eyeliner.

"In Hamundigone's case it may be true that he is a victim of the effects of the war. As for the other former liberation fighters, they have hijacked and rewritten the war story to justify their abuse and corruption. Maybe things will change when all those old men who fought in the war are gone, when we give positions on merit rather than because people were at the front together, or that they come from the same village as the leader," I said, annoyed.

"Yes, it's sad, because some of them were never in the war, they don't even know where a gun's trigger is. They were busy roasting meat in Botswana and Zambia, then, when the war ended, they come and show us scars where the meat they were enjoying burnt them, saying that they are scars from enemy bullets," Magi said, sniffing.

"What these people forget is that everyone fought in the war. The old granny with a walking stick provided chickens and goats for the boys to eat. Writers fought the war with ink. Then there were those who sang about oppression like Thomas Mapfumo, Oliver Mtukudzi, and others. The war was fought on many fronts." I said this to end the matter as I did not enjoy political discussions.

"Kundai, I'm going. I won't be here this weekend. I'm going to have fun with my old man. Let me enjoy myself before I leave life's stage. What else can I do?" she said, replacing my bottle of Cutex as she got up abruptly.

"Magi," I called as she was about to open the door and leave.

"What is it, Kundai?" she asked, smiling. Magi is very beautiful.

"Don't agree to sleep with that old man because he will simply dump you once he gets what he wants. Try to delay and see whether he is serious or, if he corners you, he should use a condom. But try by all means to avoid it and value your body." I do not know where I got the courage to speak thus.

"Thanks Kundai. But you know what? Since the time I sat down and considered the way my affairs were failing, I decided not to give my body to just anyone. So I just have fun with this old man. We can kiss and fondle but he knows that I won't go all the way. I have learnt a lesson. I will only give it to someone who is prepared to travel with me in his desire until we marry." She winked and banged the door.

This person! I kind of like her, but her head is full of water, I said to myself. I lay down and thought about life in general and what I had been discussing with Magi. As I looked at my watch to see if it was time for lunch, Magi opened my door again and said, "If my brother Vincent comes looking for me, just tell him whatever comes into your head. But I doubt he will come because he owes me money. Don't lend him any more money, Kundai. I am not leaving a message on my door because I'm not expecting anyone." She shut the door before I could answer.

I sat looking at my wristwatch, at the way the hands moved around the face. My mind was blank. I smiled to myself thinking of how ingenious the person who invented the watch was. There was a knock on my door.

"Aren't we going to the dining hall today? We'll find all the large steaks gone," Cynthia said, with just her head poking into my room.

"Let's go," I said, getting up and grabbing a ten-dollar note that lay on my desk. "I was getting carried away with my thoughts."

"Are you going to the general meeting?" Cynthia asked as we washed our hands at the tap outside the dining hall.

"No dear, I'm not coming. I have a tutorial tomorrow and I've not yet done the reading. Also Moses is coming and I don't know when he will leave," I answered, shaking my hands dry.

"Girlfriend, you are betraying the Union. But stay, it's not worth losing your boyfriend over the Union."

We laughed as we entered the dining hall.

Reuben

Mum woke up and was sick, throwing up watery white stuff. I was crying and hugged her but Charity and Sisi were holding me. Mum was also crying. She was taken to the hospital and I was left behind.

Today I am not going to the crèche because Tonderai told me that when someone is carried away in an ambulance they will be killed. I asked Aunt Charity, but she would not answer or talk to me. She just said that mum will return, but she does not want me to go and see her.

Today I would not eat their food. No one can make me unless mum is here. I want to go to my mum. Mum tells me lies that dad went to America. I know that he died. When I asked her, she admitted it and then started crying. I hate that about her. She forbids me to lie but she lies. I will tell on her to aunty at the crèche.

Unit D

No one ever thought the weather could be so bad, as if it had swallowed raw chilies and rock salt. It was dark, windy, and gloomy. The clouds were rushing eastward, whipped up by the wind. A watcher would think that there was an urgent meeting for clouds somewhere. It was so cold that mucus flowed out of noses and froze on faces, especially of those who used snuff. That day, people took out those coats that had lain in suitcases for years. The coats were creased and musty like dry stale dung. I'm certain that even pillows were degutted that day by people looking for clothes to layer. Small kids spent that day indoors. On the road, as people made their way to work, it was sniff, sniff, sniff. You'd think it was either a competition or else there was a new language. Those girls who usually walk about with their chests, thighs, and belly buttons exposed realized that the weather had put up a new law that had to be obeyed.

The sharp wind cut like a butcher's knife. Many of the roofs on the illegally built shacks in Unit D in Chitungwiza were blown off and broken up. It was fortunate that no one died, though many were injured. Where could they go? Many of them—mother, father, sisters, brothers, cousins, in-laws—all stayed in one room. These houses were not built according to any officially approved plan. Some had unfired bricks on one side, wood stolen from the industries on another, and empty fertilizer plastic bags to complete the other sides. In better examples you could see a wooden window propped open with a stick. The shacks were made up of a variety of materials, like the various ingredients that go into making a cake. The main thing for these people was to just have somewhere to sleep.

The chilly July wind had followed a heavy rainy season. I don't think even Chaminuka, who was said to have lived in Chitungwiza, ever experienced such blustery cold weather. Unit D was so overpopulated that those who lived in the posh Harare suburbs might not believe that this was Zimbabwe, if they were to pay a visit. Unit D was a disaster waiting to happen. Some even think that's what the "D" in Unit D stands for. However, disasters are the things that give the place character. Why, one of my drunk friends said that there's nothing good beginning with "D," except perhaps "darling." He gave "donkey," "dirt," "disease," and "death" as examples. Unfortunately, people laughed then and he got no chance to finish explaining his theory. True enough, there's nothing that you might seek and fail to find in Unit D. Everything is found there, and that is probably why the people who live there like it.

The footpaths in this location are usually full of people, but on that chilly windy day they were empty. There was only an occasional pedestrian here and there—no one wanted to stop and chat on their way. Only those with a mission were abroad, and if you saw anyone not wearing a jersey, then it meant they really did not have one. The vegetable vendors were not to be seen at their usual places, all that was visible were their makeshift tables, which had been blown over by the wind. Many of these tables had been snatched by small boys with ashy faces that resembled donkeys that had been rolling in the dust. These crude tables were free firewood to warm themselves on such a cold day

Litter seemed to be the only thing enjoying itself as it played tag in the wind. The wind went vhuu-uu-uu-uu-whiiii-iiii-iii, then litter flew up and floated around like swallows before a downpour. Trees contributed their share to the litter, dropping leaves on the road and rooftops, even inside houses. The leaves went in mixed with grit and bits of grass and settled as they pleased willy-nilly.

On this day, Mai Tanya suffered and cursed her ancestors and God because of her life. Saba had not been home for three days, since the day he got paid. Going to report the matter to the police was pointless, since she knew that he was OK. He had just gone to enjoy himself and squander his money. Her lips were dry and cracked with hunger, and Tanya was crying endlessly despite eating half a loaf of bread. She must have felt pain somewhere. Her mother gave her some prayer water, which she had been given by Mapostori who gathered in the open next to a busy road. The owner of the shack Mai Tanya rented had come asking for his money as the month had ended and this was now a new month. Mai Tanya explained her problems about Saba being absent.

"Ah, that's not my business. All I want is my money. It's not a problem for me to get another tenant as soon as I chuck you out," the landlord said, biting a cigarette.

The shack he was threatening to expel them from had long since rotted; it was a home only for want of a better word. Those who could afford dogs would not even allow their dogs to sleep in such a shack. The shacks were built in a chain that went on and on like a train track.

Mai Tanya had had enough of the shack and her life with Saba. She had tried selling freezits when he was at work to raise bus fare to return back home to Jerera. What she would do once she got there was no longer of great concern to her. She thought it better to be killed by her own father rather than by a stranger who not only had not paid lobola for her but, furthermore, cared nothing for her. She felt under the mattress to retrieve her bus money hidden there. She was tempted to use the money to pay the rent and buy mealie meal, but she resisted. She knew that she might find herself in hot soup for that when Saba came. He would say there was no food here when he left, so where had the food come from? She knew him well. Her heart was set on fending for Tanya and herself in the future. She pulled the money from the mattress and gently unrolled it as if she feared that the money might just take off. After counting it, Mai Tanya found it to be $67.40. Having paid off the initial loan that VC had given her for start-up capital, she felt free to go. She decided that the only person she would bid farewell would be VC. She wanted to wait for Saba to return so that she would see him one last time and then leave as soon as he went to work. But, whether he came or not, she was determined to go back home early the next morning. She watched her child drowsing and it warmed her heart; she smiled a little and sighed.

For now, mother and daughter were in the dark. They usually had candles in their shack, but they had used them up the previous night. Tanya finally slept. Her mother sat huddled in the dark. She felt a sudden ache in her stomach as if she were being cut up. Her period was not due, so it was likely to be something else. The wind had broken down her door, which was made from an old oil drum, and she used a log to hold it up. The gusts passed through the gaps in the shack and the roofing material responded with squeaks. Mai Tanya listened to the wind whistling and the debris carried in the wind striking her roof like hail. She tried to get up to close the worst hole but failed, as she had a bad cramp in one of her legs. She moaned and panted in the dark as Tanya slept. Mai Tanya reached for her thin jersey, which lay on her plank bed, and put it on as she sat and listened to people outside who were shouting to make themselves heard above the wind.

If she had relatives in Harare she might have gone to stay with them but, sadly, the only relatives in the city were her man's. In any case, in Harare, no one likes to support another. Plus, she could not go to them without her man. Leaving a man is a big problem that women face. If she was educated it would have been easier to look after herself, but, as it was, her life had been entirely in Saba's hands. Mai Tanya felt tears and wiped them away with the back of her hand. She felt a sharp pain in her side, which made her curl up and cry as she tried to reach for the door and remove the log to call for help. As she was feeling for the log she heard footsteps outside the door. The person outside tried to open the door, but the log inside held firm.

"Hey you dog, open up the door!" Saba shouted, banging on the door. No one answered him. "You snake! Open the door. Why sit in the dark, are you a witch? Open the door before I kick you." He was smashed.

Mai Tanya tried to answer but failed to say a thing. The pain was now crushing everything: her head, her stomach, her chest, her eyes. Her ears were ringing and she felt dizzy.

"You daughter of a witch, I never did marry you so don't be so arrogant in there. Why do you sleep at nine, are you sick? By the time you open that door I'll be ready to kill you. You know me well."

As Mai Tanya was struggling up, the door was kicked in. It cut her belly, while the log that had been supporting the door knocked her in the head. She groaned once and gasped, "Father of Tanya, look after my child, you have murdered me."

Saba entered the room, stepping over his wife, then fell down somewhere near where Tanya was sleeping next to the pots. The child began to cry.

"Dammit, be quiet Tanya. This is your Daddy. Hey, Mai Tanya, get up and pick up the baby, she's crying," he said, feeling along the bed.

"Where are the matches?" He searched in one of his pockets.

The whole room reeked of beer.

Saba found the matches and lit one to light the room. What he saw sobered him up at once. He stood there staring like a witch caught by an unexpected dawn. The burnt down matchstick scorched his fingers and brought him to himself. Tanya screamed when she saw her mother.

"On no. What have I done? Mai Tanya, my wife, please get up." Sweat broke out from all his pores.

He fled from the room and left the infant crying in the dark. Once outside he thought of telling his landlord but found it too hard. He set off for VC's place instead. He was nervous and jumpy when he got there and did not bother to knock but simply opened the door and went in.

"Sekuru Saba," VC said, getting up from the bed where he sat with a girl. "Now you are—"

Saba gave him no time to finish his sentence.

"VC, I've just killed my wife," Saba said, covering his face with his hands. If VC had not seen blood on Saba's hands and trousers he might have refused to believe him.

Saba immediately ran out into the gusting wind. By the time VC came out he had already gone, God alone knows where. VC ran to Saba's room and what he saw there floored him. Tanya cried incessantly, with no one to console her, and the gathered crowd looked on in horror.

Bunny

I am trying to remember the story that Charity told me this morning on the kombi to town. I can't because I am simply exhausted. My eyes are heavy from lack of sleep. What did Charity say? What's surprising is how I could forget. I am always sleepy these days. I don't understand and I am not happy anymore.

Perhaps there is a ngozi or something behind it, as if I murdered someone and their spirit is back to haunt me. If I was certain about what those of the Mapostori sects do, perhaps I would go there and ask for a prayer, but these people are all dubious. In Harare, life is only about conning each other. Everyone is just looking for ways to make money. I will not waste money paying for services in which I have no trust. VC told me that some of the Mapostori actually come to him to buy mbanje. I wait to see what parcel fate will deliver; if I go mad, so be it.

Bedtime brings me so much fear. I am having meaningless dreams. Shards of dreams. Incoherent dreams. I drink so I can forget and sleep well, but it is not working. Yesterday, when I took the car for servicing, I asked for a day off at work because everything has become meaningless. I have a faint headache. I don't feel quite myself. Not that I am sick. I think about AIDS, Maud's death, and whether I too might have HIV. Yesterday I thought I might be able to sleep but that night was the longest I have ever been through. And today I was somewhere between sleep and wakefulness, turning over and over like a worm on its back trying to right itself so that it can crawl again. I suffered. I sat up in bed though my eyes were fighting against a week of insomnia. I don't know how I fell asleep sitting up on the bed like that. The dream I had was not a good one.

I was in a long clearing without grass or trees or birds. I could not see where it ended. I was walking barefoot even though there were sharp stones. I staggered along, sometimes crawling. The clearing changed into a pool full of deep, dark water. Across the pool were slim, tall, fair girls bathing. They called me, saying that they wanted to wash me as I was filthy. But I saw no way of getting to where they were bathing. So they walked over the water and took my hands to lead me back to where they had been. In the middle of the pool I slipped from their hands and sank into the water. As I sank I saw Maud holding a plate with gourd-shaped squashes, which she was eating raw. When she saw me she gave me some and told me to eat. As I was about to eat they transformed into baby crocodiles. Maud, who was now on the other side of the pool, shouted at me to watch out for the crocodiles. When I tried to flee toward her, she turned into a mass of slime. A crocodile grabbed my head and tried to swallow me. As I was fighting it we sank into the mud and the crocodile changed into a policeman. He clutched my throat and threatened to kill me unless I told him where my younger brother VC kept his stash of ganja. I wanted to say I did not know but the policeman pushed me deeper into the mire and I sank further. Everything went dark. I tried to get out and felt the mud change to a veil. I was marrying Mai Jazz, Maud's elder sister. When we were about to kiss I saw her mouth was full of blood and she had fangs like a lion. That is when I came awake screaming. Charity was knocking on my door asking if I was going to work today. I'm still frazzled by that dream.

The dreams are all similar. I don't understand it. They lie heavy on me. Even so, they are better than those I had in the three previous days. Imagine dreaming that you are fighting with God. Even now when I think about it, it gives me the creeps. Though I am not a churchgoer, I fear God, and I know that he is the Almighty, but I had those dreams on three consecutive nights—fighting with God. In the dreams, I sought God to dare him but I found myself alone, God nowhere in sight. It was just me holding a pick and a shovel, digging a grave in an anthill. I am scared that, if I have this dream again, I will surely go mad. Not crazy like Hamundigone but really insane, running down the street stark naked. I had never sweated in the mind before. My mind sweated until it was numb. Now it has a rash that itches without respite. I can feel death stalking me like a hunter who has hit an animal that has left a bloody trail.

I am tired of worrying. I no longer fear death; if it comes, let it come. It will find me here. No one wants to die, but everything that flies will eventually perch. After all, that which doesn't come to an end is threateningly inauspicious. There is nothing to fear since all of us will die one day. It could be today, tomorrow, or next week. Those who died with unfinished plans did not want to die, but they had no choice, as death had come upon them. It is futile to resist certain things. Why, even when children play hopscotch or nhodo they will eventually be out. Even if they cheat or pretend that they are not out, they have to be out sometime. I don't quite recall now since I haven't been to church in a while, but I think it must be in Ecclesiastes where it says there is a time for everything, a time to sow, a time to reap. So if I die from AIDS I will just say it was destiny. So I won't trouble myself. I will wait and see; I suspect that I could be infected, but I have not had any blood tests. I examined myself in the mirror this morning to see whether there is any truth in what people have been saying, that I have lost weight. It seems true. It seems to me that my cheeks are slightly sunken. I don't know if that is it, we'll see. My time will have come. Sometimes we make life difficult for ourselves. If we would only listen to the awareness campaigns and see the way people are dying. In any case no one ever does something with the intention of seeking death. My mind is tired now. Let me go to the little bar at the Ambassador Hotel and drink whisky or vodka, maybe I might feel better. Tonight when I go to bed I want to be ready for all these dreams that have been frightening me. I want to think of them as I sleep, wait for them. If I don't dream, then I will seek them until I find them, because they are trying to drive me crazy. I am going to sleep like nobody's business. I don't care anymore; the dreams want to be with me. So I will simply wait until they come. If I am dead come morning, so be it. Anyway, I have realized that life is boring because I don't even know what I want. There is nothing new. It is the same stuff everyday:

Waking up, bathing, eating, walking.
Spending the day talking, laughing, sulking,
Walking, eating, sleeping, dreaming,
Waking, tiring, thinking, tiring,
Eating, defecating, walking, being bored,
Being troubled, sitting, wooing and being wooed,
Being loved, being rejected, being fearful, seeking knowledge,
Growing, seeing and seeing and seeing,
Grieving, lamenting, weeping, brooding,

Forgetting, walking, talking,
Showing off, boasting,
Seeking, not finding, finding, not finding,
Lodging, letting, evicting, being angry,
Drunkenness, confusion, regretting,
Being at a loss, being irritated, walking,
Returning, seeing, brooding, fearing,
Eating, chatting, words, bad words,
Lying to each other, scaring each other, pleasing each other,
Promises, expectancy, dreaming, losing out,
Sleeping, seeing, waking, working,
Knowing, pretending to know and understanding,
Living, making do, trying,
Fearing, not sleeping, brooding, agonizing.

The pattern is an ant's journey,
Going and coming back, circling and circling.
It is hard to understand how it goes,
Ladies never swap it.

Life is a weeded plot
Where weeds sprout again tomorrow
And the day after
Until life is no more.
All you have harvested being only questions.

If it could be escaped
You would catch me having passed Nehanda and other long-gone ancestors
By uncountable strides
Because here on earth I don't know,
I don't know what I want anymore!

What am I saying? Am I now mad?

Magi

I have never suffered the way I do these days. That is what motivated me to bring the matter to court. I am emotionally roasting like a pig on a spit. It is impossible for me to forgive Mangwiro. If only he did not come to my dreams raping me again and again, I would let it rest, but I am sorely troubled. I have flashes of him wrestling me down. And in these visions, he doesn't come bearing his own face. The body and clothes are his, but he has a twisted face like that of a tokoloshi. I don't really know what a tokoloshi looks like but what I see has left me feeling like food that has been chewed and spat out.

I wonder why I kept quiet. Perhaps if I had told Kundai about it when we were still in college she would have helped me in some way. I left it too long. I left it like a boil, which is now full of throbbing pus that needs me to find someone to lance it. I terminated the pregnancy but it did not help. What he did to me won't leave me. It was not expelled with the fetus. I thought mum would help me, but she didn't. Sometimes we women let each other down.

When we came out of the court Mangwiro asked to speak to me briefly. He asked me to be understanding about the matter and stop condemning him. We could do an out-of-court settlement, he suggested. He wanted me to say he did not rape me.

"Shamwari, look, I have a family that needs looking after. Besides, I don't even know if my job will still be open to me." He was pitiable.

I did not reply. Mukoma Bunny was waiting for me in his car so we could go. I just told him, "Sorry, the leopard is fine when dragging others, but when it gets dragged, it says my spots are full of dust. I can't help you. I nearly died aborting your pregnancy, so how many times do you want me to die?"

"Magi, please," he said, on the verge of tears, seeing that I had turned my back on him to go. I looked at his wife standing by their car and felt sorry for her, but I did not consider agreeing to his request, as he could do it again. He has no shame, Mangwiro. Did my brother VC not say respect those who respect you and despise those who despise you? That is what it is here in Harare. If we were kumusha I might fear a feud.

Mukoma Bunny hooted to call me. We have to go and see Vincent at his lodgings. It is said he was beaten up by the landlord's daughter and her husband. He is badly hurt but at the hospital they did not admit him as there were no beds available.

"What was Mangwiro saying?" Mukoma Bunny asked me.

"He's a sick man that one. He sees that there is no way out for him and is asking for an out-of-court settlement," I answered shyly. It is not proper to discuss issues like being raped with one's brother. So I quickly changed the topic.

"What happened with Sekuru Saba's case?" I asked.

"That is a big one. He was found guilty and sentenced to life. He tried to appeal but the fact that he often used to beat his partner close to death meant the case went against him. He was also heard saying that he would kill Mai Tanya by those in the neighboring shack."

"Sentencing him to life in prison is useless because Saba is not a healthy man. What will happen to Tanya?"

"Saba's sister from Zviyambe took her and said she would look after her."

"She really helped a poor soul. I have heard about this Zviyambe one, but I have never met her." There was silence for a while.

Then I wanted to hear more about Vincent. "How come Vincent was attacked?"

He cleared his throat then scratched his cheek. "It's said that when we went to Maud's funeral . . . you know, don't you, that Mai Jazz is Maud's elder sister? I didn't, I only realized this when we met at the hospital. When we were at the funeral with Mai Jazz, Heaven, her daughter, is said to have beaten up the maid and stripped her, then chased her outside in the nude. So this girl, I think she is called Sarudzai, sought refuge in Vincent's room. VC then took up the issue. It seems Saru had told VC about Heaven's husband before. He used to force Saru to sleep with him, threatening dire consequences if she told anyone. Saru, fearing Mai Jazz and her daughter, kept quiet about it. It is said both mother and daughter have a temper that seems demonic. Also, they say Saru was saving money for her brother kumusha to write his O-levels. She could not leave because she had worked for five months without any pay, Mai Jazz telling her that she would pay her in one go. Saru found herself in a situation in which she no longer knew what to do."

"Ah, Mukoma, do you mean to tell me that this son-in-law, who you call Heaven's partner, lives at his mother-in-law's house?" I asked.

"He lives at his mother-in-law's and he is unemployed. Just imagine," Bunny replied, changing gears.

I don't know whether Bunny is growing old. These days he is very quiet. Maybe it is because of his landlady's death. But should one grieve over a landlady's death as if one has lost a girlfriend?

"So was VC beaten for defending the girl?" I wanted to hear more.

"Heaven and her husband demanded that VC throw the whore out of his room and he refused. Then he started berating Heaven and her husband. I'm told he said, 'You should not abuse people simply because they come from kumusha.' He said no one was to touch Saru. Heaven was fuming and wanted to fight VC. VC slapped her. It's then that she screamed and started fighting VC, scratching him. At that stage her husband came with a shovel and hit VC on the head with it. The couple then beat him until he passed out. He only regained consciousness at the hospital. After assaulting VC they rushed to the police station to report that he had sacks of mbanje in his room."

"They are witches," I said, pained.

"If it were not for VC's girlfriend, Joyi, he would be in prison now because there was a lot of mbanje in his room that had just been delivered."

"And what did this girl do?"

"This girl sometimes shacks up with VC, sometimes she's thrown out, then they get back together, and so it goes. She arrived after the fight was over and was told that those who had thrashed VC had gone to the police. She went into his room and saw the sacks of mbanje from Malawi. She made a quick plan and called Sanchez, VC's friend, who drives kombis. They removed the mbanje so that when the police arrived they found nothing. They then arrested Heaven and her husband, charging them with assault."

"Why, it was quite some drama," I said, picturing VC in my mind.

"Your brother is too headstrong. He won't listen. How long do you think he will last selling mbanje and surviving through luck like that? He'll rot in jail where Saba is, because if he is ever caught with so much mbanje in his possession, there is no option of a fine or any way out. Now he is asking me to hide his mbanje at my house, but I told him I won't do it. I'd lose my job if I were arrested. Talk to him when we get there."

"I will talk to him, Mukoma."

Bunny does not know that I used to get customers for VC from among the boys at university. If he discovers this he will be very upset.

"So what is the school you are going to teach at called?" he asked, looking at me.

"It's called Nyakasikana in Mount Darwin."

"Now hunozi people are going to be found in the reserve." Bunny laughed at me.

"Am I a munozi?" I asked, surprised that he sees me as one.

"Yes, you eat at Nando's and speak English with an accent. And your fashion taste is overwhelming evidence that you are a munozi. Look at your shoes," he replied, smiling.

"Ha, brother, you are mistaken. Eating at Nando's, yes, but speaking English with an accent, no. Of course I dress fashionably to move with the times," I said, laughing too.

"Now when you go to Nyakasikana the harsh sun will make your skin dark, and when you come back to Harare you will be speaking with a Korekore accent. How come some of your mates are getting jobs in Harare?"

"It's because they have uncles or other relatives at those workplaces, Mukoma."

"We were given someone to train in our department called Kundai Mahachi. How can someone who did English honors do auditing? It would have been better if she had done accounts or business studies."

"Who did you say? Kundai is now at your workplace? No, that's not possible. It's impossible." I was astounded.

"What, you know her?" Bunny asked.

"We lived on the same corridor at university. I know her. I would really like to see her before I go to Nyakasikana. How did she do it? Is it possible? Kundai!"

"You can come and see her, but she won't take you to lunch. She started only three weeks ago."

"Lunch is something else, Mukoma. I only want to chat with her about life. She's a very nice girl and I wouldn't mind if you told me she's my sister-in-law," I said, to needle him.

He did not reply, then he laughed and said, "She's too skinny and she's too munozi."

"Ah, Kundai has always been like that, as if she's malnourished. As for English, she likes it so much that she carries it to the extreme at times. But Mukoma, you did not tell me what happened to your girlfriend from Solusi? That one is a real munozi, unlike people like us who stink of sweat." Finally, I had asked him what I really wanted to ask.

"It simply cooled down, you know. Sometimes I don't understand how a person you love so much that you can't sleep suddenly becomes the one you hate the most. I don't know how the fire that blazed between us went cold. I think I was so oblivious to the wall that had come up between us that I failed to notice it when we stopped doing the little things that we had always done for each other. It kept creeping higher all the time. I felt better when she was at university. I thought things would improve. She wrote me a letter. Here, let me give it to you so you can read for yourself. I don't know why I've kept it." He sighed and shook his head. He handed me a letter written on blue note paper. It bore no address or date. It simply said:

Dear Bunny

I thought I would write to you and tell you what I think about love. I'm not lecturing you, but simply telling you my opinion.

The way we fell in love was hasty, like an ambulance arriving at an accident scene. I know that I tried to be in love with you when I was neither committed nor settled. I fell in love with you for reasons that can hardly sustain a love. I just needed a pillar to lean on, something like a ride to get me to where I wanted to go. What I did not know is that true love comes from the heart of hearts, from deep within. I was just emerging from depression after breaking up with my long-time boyfriend, my first lover. I think I just threw myself at you without much thought. I just needed a tree under whose shade I could rest—not that I cared what kind of tree it was, a muhacha, a mususu, a muvanga, or a mango tree. I went and sat beneath it to rest. Now my mind has recovered and I feel refreshed. I am now myself. But let me tell you the things that put me off you. If it were not for them, I might have tried to learn to love you with all my heart, but it is no longer possible.

First, when it is your girl's birthday, don't think of this day like any other day. Make time to take her out for dinner, to a good place where you can talk, and give her a present. I won't tell you about what happened on my birthday, you know it. I won't repeat it because I might just cry from frustration. You don't live with Dynamos Football Club; maybe if they had won the match you went to watch on my birthday, it might have made up for it.

Bunny, I know you grew up in the rural areas, but you should ask others when you don't know how to go about certain things. You embarrassed me the day I invited you home for dinner. You came dressed like a tsotsi. If you still remember, you wore a T-shirt, jeans, and a cap. I would understand if I had told you to dress casually. What you did showed that you did not respect or attach importance to my home, my parents, or me. That was not the only time you have done this. One day you took me to dinner dressed in a jacket and T-shirt with animal designs. I did not say anything, thinking it would change. If you dislike wearing a tie just wear your shirt buttoned to the top.

Then there's the tie that's not at all suitable for work. You know the tie with the Mickey Mouse cartoon on it. That tie is not at all suitable for work, it makes you look like a cartoon yourself. Your style of dressing is infuriating at times. I'll leave the matter alone now lest you take it personally and think I am insulting you.

I like you, Bunny. You are smart and ambitious but if only you would stop drinking and supporting Dynamos Football Club as though the team were your mother and father or even the very air you breathe. As for beer, I guess you were already drinking when I met you, but I don't know why you do it because you gain nothing from it except degradation. Beware of your drinking lest it make you unmarriageable.

Let me stop here. Don't forget to invite me to your wedding.

Have a nice time.

Your friend
Lorna

I sighed. I wanted to laugh but stopped myself in case the recipient of the letter might think he was the object of my mirth or consider me immature. Bunny has never done such a thing before, allowing me to read a letter from his girlfriend. It seems we are becoming friends these days. He's more congenial now. The letter made me feel both pity and anger. I thought about what Jonathan had done to me at university. I must have been childish as I did not realize that the fire blazing with love was one-sided, on my side, but long cold on his. Love matters are hard because they can leave you with a tattered heart.

"So you read for yourself how she felt." Bunny spoke, bringing me back from my thoughts.

"Yeah, it's tough. Anyway, she's OK because she speaks the truth. Some people make you believe that they are still in love when love has long gone cold in their hearts. But I think that this was more of a confession to purge her soul. You know what, Mukoma B, you might do bad things to someone and then later find it hard to forget about what you did. I think that is the reason why Lorna wrote such a letter. She used you. Anyway, I won't comment on some of the things she mentions, but I think she is too fussy. Anyway, coming from a munozi, such a thing is hardly surprising."

"Things nowadays are impossible to understand. But Magi, tell me honestly and forget that I am your brother. Why are girls acting desperate in Harare? You know what, I gave a very attractive girl a lift from Harare. She has a good job in the city as a public relations officer in a hotel. We chatted about many things in general. She asked me my age and my job and I told her. When we arrived I left her in New Zengeza 4, where she was visiting her older sister, and made a date to meet at Meikles Hotel later that evening. Do you know what? I was surprised to see her bring a suitcase, but I ignored it. After dinner, when we were saying goodbye, she said that she was coming home with me. I was shocked. At first I thought she was joking but when I realized that she was serious I told her firmly it was not on."

I burst out laughing, "Is this story true, Mukoma B?"

"Do you think I'm kidding? It happened right here in Harare. It's not a story from *Kwayedza* or a pub story," he said earnestly.

"I think you might have given her the impression that she could not afford to let you slip out of her hands. I think she wanted to show you that she wanted to live with you, then let whatever would come come."

"But Magi, we did not even know each other well."

"Maybe this girl once lost the chance to be with someone she loved by playing hard to get. But also, some guys are not patient with girls who take too long to show that they are interested. So rather than lose a good catch, the girls will end up falling in love like instant coffee."

"Maybe you are right," Bunny responded lazily.

"Maybe another reason is that this girl wanted to be a successful career girl but then panicked, seeing that she was aging. That is our disadvantage as women because we are like products that have a shelf life. Once past a certain stage they become useless. How old did she say she was?"

"I did not ask, but she appeared to be about my age. It's just that women are good at concealing their age because of the South African cosmetics they use," he said, glancing at me.

"Maybe you had mentioned to her that you wanted to get married?"

"I told her that if I found the right person whom I loved and who had a good job, I would marry her at once," he answered as we stopped at traffic lights.

"Ah, so she must have thought you meant her?"

"Yeah, I think it could be that conversation that did it because her behavior was astonishing. But I never said it was her. It was hard for me to think she was a prostitute because she—"

"No Mukoma B, she's not a prostitute. Prostitutes do it for money, but she is educated and has a good job. She was serious and liked you." I spoke sincerely. I think that he is old enough to settle down and get married.

"So, if you have many things to carry, please tell me. Then I can plan to take you to your Nyakasikana school," he said, changing the topic.

"That would be helpful. You know when you go to a new place you have to be well equipped rather than borrowing things from neighbors. They might hex you."

"Um-m Magi, don't fear witchcraft like VC. You will find that the people there might be even better than those in Harare. So long as you don't fall for the mudhibhisi." He laughed at me.

"Maybe you might want to keep cattle one day and you will have a brother-in-law who knows about dipping them," I said, laughing too, but I got the message. "So come home when you are packed and fetch me so that we can collect your goods. That will allow me to see my girl Rudo," Bunny said, pulling at his beard.

"So how long will you continue staying at Maud's place?" I asked.

"I don't know, there's a new landlord now, her brother who was once a teacher but was fired because of insanity. He is the new owner of the house."

I was shocked. Someone who was a teacher and fired because of madness? Is it possible my brother no longer remembers Hamundigone? Surely he was there when Hamundigone came to pay damages? But I suppose since he only saw Hamundigone that once he has now forgotten him. Could it be him? I'll see for myself when I go there. But what will I do if it is him? You never know with madmen. But if it is him, I want to talk to him and see for myself whether it is true that he is crazy.

"Why are you so quiet, as if you were having your hair cut?" Bunny's voice startled me.

We had arrived at the Chitungwiza town center and were entering Unit D.

VC and Joyi

"But Joyi, just tell me one thing that might convince me that this baby you're carrying is mine. I don't like things that disrupt my business. Do you hear? I know you looked after me when I was injured, but why should I keep you now? Because of the pregnancy? That's your problem. Do you hear me?"

"VC, how can you say that?"

"Why not? Are you the First Lady? I don't care. I want you gone when I come back." He banged the door and it fell off its hinges.

"Oh no, what will Mai Jazz say?" he said, picking up the door.

Mai Jazz came out of her house shouting, "Am I to be left with anything intact in this house?"

Charity

Sekuru Hamundigone came yesterday, drunk and reeking of sweat. His clothes were damp as if he had fallen in water. I don't know. He arrived at three in the morning when we were all asleep and woke me up to play him a cassette that he always carries around with him by Thomas Mapfumo called *Gwindingwi rine Shumba*. I refused to get up, and he did it himself, putting the volume on at full blast. He played a song that went:

Nharo hapana, tiri kutonga isu
Tose vatema
Takazviudzwa naVaMugabe
Zanu nevanhu, Zanu chiiko?
Zanu vanhu, vanhu iZanu . . .

There's no doubt, we are ruling
All of us Blacks
We were told this by Mr. Mugabe
Zanu and the people, what is Zanu?
Zanu is the people and the people are Zanu . . .

He started crying. He woke Reuben up to tell him a folktale. I tried to reason with him, telling him to let the child sleep, but he looked at me with eyes full of broken bottles. Imagine Sekuru Hamundigone waking up the child just to tell him a useless story about owl and other birds.

"Reuben, a long time ago, when birds could talk, Owl was the leader of all the birds. Owl was the leader, as he was the only one of all the birds with horns, but he misused his horns. He made all the birds worship him, sing for him, and get his food. He used his horns to threaten any bird that did not bring him food. But the truth is that what other birds believed to be horns were really tufts of feathers.

"After many years working for Owl, singing for him and feeding him, the birds became sick of it. One day as Owl was holding a meeting with the other birds, Blackbird went to sit near Owl and watched him closely. He saw that what Owl called horns were actually feathers. He refused to forage for Owl and the other birds were amazed. Owl said to Blackbird, 'I'll get you with my horns.'

"Blackbird replied, 'You have no horns at all, just feathers you threaten us with. From today onward your life of luxury is over.'

"Blackbird started pecking at Owl and pulling out the feathers that Owl had claimed to be horns. Owl howled and fled and all the birds were happy.

"You know what, Reuben, that's why owls only fly at night while other birds fly in the daytime. Sleep now, my nephew, because you're no owl."

Magi

Saba died the day before yesterday. He hanged himself in his jail cell. I did not attend his funeral. Those who attended said it was not a funeral but a nhamo. At a funeral people sit on sofas and drink beer and the deceased is in a casket. But with Saba there was nothing at all. Even the coffin was a problem until Mukoma Bunny and company bought one. For some, poverty follows them to the grave.

Bunny

We were drinking beer with Hamundigone on the veranda when a small white feather blown by the wind floated down. It blew around in the air then landed on Hamundigone's shoe. He picked it up off his shoe, which was unglued at the front, looking like a fish that's about to swallow a hook. He held it in two fingers and blew it away to continue on its journey. It rose into the air, spun, and landed on him again. It landed on his shoulder like a rare badge. He took it and placed it in his pocket without looking at it. A small white feather. I don't know if it came off a flying bird or a domestic broiler chicken. I wondered why he put it in his pocket.

I now accept him just as he is. It's hard for me to say whether he is mad because some of the things he says are true and significant, but the way he talks is confusing, so it is hard to say he is sane. In one conversation he said, "Bunny, do you know that I don't sleep? It depends, when I am drunk I do, but mostly I don't sleep. I constantly hear war songs in my head. Does that happen to you too, hearing songs in your head?"

I was shocked thinking about the song "*Kwasara kunesu*," which haunts my nights and prevents my sleep. I did not wish to tell him about that. I remained quiet.

"Do you ever hear a rebel in your head that tells you to stop the police at a roadblock from stopping cars? A rebel who says, go to the president's home and say I've come to eat sadza with you today. Bunny, in my head are songs that will not be silenced. They go then return. I try to pen them up in an alcoholic cage, but they escape when I am not drunk. But this does not mean that I am saying I am mad. If I'm to be mad it will happen in the future, for now I am fully rational.

"I am not mad, but I know those who are mad. We know those who are mad. It is those who claim to have fought in the war of liberation when they did not. They are mad those leaders who claim that they saw too much bloodshed during the war of liberation and want to offer libations of more blood. The madmen are those who see madness in others when they cannot see their own. Madmen are those who do not want to be reproached that they are being selfish. Madmen are you and me, Bunny, who smile at the selfish acts of fools. The madmen tear up children's clothes to make up their suits. They have cataracts in their eyes, not natural ones but cataracts that cause them to see mirages and fail to fix problems. You say I am mad but I say it is you who are mad. Which of us is really mad?"

He became silent. Playing on the radio was a song that Maud used to sing for me. My heart skipped a beat. Hamundigone started talking again, "There are endless numbers of madmen. The mad are seen through their madness like those youths, who, when they are helped up into a tall tree so they can pick the wild fruit, will eat from the tree and only throw down pips at those below. Bunny, am I mad? If I am, tell me so that I can get down from that tree. I don't want to fall down from that tree. I want to come down and receive thanks for having dropped fruit to others. I don't want them to laugh at my scratches but for them to appreciate that I was wounded on their behalf. I don't want to continue beating the drum after people have stopped dancing because I am not a madman.

"One's downfall may come from a seemingly insignificant source. When you see water dripping from the baboon's brow then you know it has been drizzling for a long time. Let us be human. People who are happy only if another is happy. We are human beings, but sometimes animals are better than us.

Sometimes I don't understand; maybe I'm aging or really mad, but I don't understand. If one thinks only they are special, and all others are merely crumbs, it's worrying," he said, pulling the feather from his pocket and looking at it. It had bits of peanut skins stuck to it from his pocket. He blew at the feather and laughed as one who has seen someone milking a dog.

"How does it happen that we fail to see that there are many of us in the family? Why do we not listen to each other? What makes us think that other people's opinions are less important than ours? What makes us boast about the beauty of our wives, about our large salaries, about how boring one of our six cars is to drive so that we want to look for a car that is more fun? What is it? What makes us want to talk about the places where we drink, the political parties we support, the soccer teams that we follow as though those to whom we are boasting do not have stories about their own drinking places or the intelligence of their children? Every person went to school somewhere and has a favorite drinking place, and if we were to listen to all of their stories it would be too tedious. Bunny, let us grow up in the way we talk and think.

"It's said that he who screams longs to be heard, but don't scream for no reason, as screams annoy others. People here in Harare ought not to do that. Just like Dynamos supporters who, when Dembare wins, won't go to work and expect everyone else to celebrate because Dembare is the only team. They say whoever does not like Dembare will be smashed, that they will thrash them to silence, clobber them until they are Dembare fans."

I was amused, seeing as I am a Dembare fan. I didn't agree with him but I kept my silence. What does it matter after all?

"Dembare supporters are hardheaded and tyrannical. But was it not us who said down with tyranny? Hm-m-m? Did we not say forward with harmony? If we argue for the national team to only carry Dembare players, it won't go well. We need a cross-fertilization of talent from other teams' aces so that our national team is strong. But when you are like a Dembare fan who is blind to the talent in other teams then you are among the walking dead. Your mind is deformed. It is madness!"

He brought out his goat's horn snuff container and shook it before opening it to get some snuff.

"Never fear, Bunny, for at the end of the day everything returns. Everything returns to its source like dust to dust and ashes to ashes, or like baboons when they have finished reaping where they did not sow and return to the mountains. The same happens in the industrial areas where overalls are folded away and bicycle tires pumped up. The workers will return home where they came from.

"Dashing to crowd against each other at the minibuses, mothers feel their breasts heavy with milk for their babies who spent the day in the care of their maids. Everything, Bunny, returns. Even the kombis, no matter how fast, will, at the end of the day, be parked, the engines switched off, and the hwindis will count their money and go home to sleep. So give things time, man. But whoever has stolen, let him not steal from now on, but let him toil with his hands and produce good that he might give to the one who is in need. All these tall stories about fighting in the liberation war must end. I came from kumusha when I went to war so that is where I want to return. Do you hear me, Bunny?" He growled the last words, his red eyes glaring. I simply nodded my head like a kid being sent on an errand to the shops.

"Struggling is now my garb, as if I were never ambitious. People think I am mad. Heaven, my sister's child, turned me out of their home the way she does with their dog, Harare. Her mother, my sister, says nothing. She is terrified of her own child as though she were a CIO operative. I thought Cleodia was mine but she snubbed me. The only person who seemed to love me was my sister, the late Maud. There is nothing and no one for me. Now look at me bent over like a shitting dog. This is aging, isn't it? I've been conned, I know the ones who conned me but it's OK. I came back from the war after seven years with nothing except for these scars. Today they call me comrade but I feel like crying because, by the time I came back, what I fought for had been eaten by jackals.

"Do you know that our maiguru is difficult?" he asked, looking at me. I wondered which sister-in-law this was and what she had to do with the subject under discussion, so I merely nodded my head.

He took up the story again, "My sister-in-law is difficult, like arrogant Kaitano whom the comrades beat up at Mukumbura. Everything has an ending—did not Chimbetu say 'Kutuka kwavanoita kuchapera, hapana dunhu risina rinda—All their badmouthing will come to an end because we all die'? Do you know that song of Chimbetu's? It is called "Hope iyi." Chimbetu is damn good. If he were my younger brother, I would buy him a sweet that never finishes, not bubble gum but a real sweet. I love Chimbetu. Do you know, even if my sister-in-law is like that, Mukoma Ruka does not notice it? Even when he sees it, he does nothing about it. So why should I stay in their house? I wanted Charity and Reuben to go and stay at their house but realized it wouldn't do. It's not suitable for me or them. If she attended our funerals, you might have seen her, but she did not come to Maud's funeral. Only mukoma came and he said she was away. She enjoys her huge house in Gunhill. They don't die where they live, hence they don't attend others' funerals. They have knocked down poverty with a knobkerrie while we strive with it as though it was bequeathed to us by Smith at the death of Rhodesia.

"Hey, Charity, listen to the backing voice on that Biggie Tembo song playing, she sounds just like my sister Maud. Can't you hear it? Oh, why do these things happen?"

And here I am trying to forget about Maud; I don't even want to think about her. What's the old man doing now?

"By the way, what did you say about your maiguru?" I asked, to divert him from the discussion on Maud that he was about to start.

"Maiguru is a tough nut. As for me, she does not love me at all, yet I am her brother's blood. I saw it as far back as their wedding, that she would give us juju to make us ineffectual. As soon as I said it, she screamed murder, she said that all of us hated her and she knew it. She accused us of loving our brother's former wife. How could we not love her if she treated us properly, Bunny?

Ask Mai Jazz and she will tell you how well our other maiguru, who is now divorced, treated us. At this one's wedding she scowled at us so much that I looked around to see if there were any sewage pipes burst nearby. She accused us of not bringing any gifts and that we merely came to eat. I said maiguru, where would we get the money?

"But I'm afraid maiguru was angry, particularly when I became drunk. After all, I am unaccustomed to whisky. I didn't know whether whisky was to be drunk by the bottle or not and so, when I got the chance, I drank it like nobody's business because I thought it was a special drink since I only saw it being drunk by chefs. Please forgive me for that, maiguru, please indulge me. I will even destroy the empty bottle that I took home and filled with tea to make it look as if it still contains whisky. Even those who filched food and money need your forgiveness because they love you. That is why they were at the wedding. The idea was not to steal; they absent-mindedly took them on their way out. Forgive, maiguru, they are unthinking. I know them. But those who took the leftovers don't have any dogs to feed; they were saving the food to eat the following day.

"Bunny, if you want to go to maiguru's, talk to Charity so that she can go with you and you'll see it for yourself. The last day I was there I left her shouting at her kid for eating bread without egg or bacon. That is our maiguru."

He laughed, then got up to go to the toilet. I thought about what he was saying. I can't quite put it together into a consistent picture but one day I will. I'll ask Charity. Now my mind won't flow well, a bit like water that has flowed into a hole. It can't flow out because there's nowhere to run. I'm tired. I think I will soon be like Hamundigone. Two mad men. I laughed drunkenly. I don't know whether it was drunkenness from the beer or from mental strain.

"You see, young man," he said, adjusting his chair so he could sit more comfortably. "I am now old, actually turning forty-eight next month, but I had nothing to my name. Now I have things because of the legacy left by my sister. Look, they fired me saying

I am mad, but I'm not mad. I know that. I have no idea where this came from. If they had sent me to a psychiatrist and he confirmed it I would accept it. But to base this on the fact that I was no longer teaching the kids the authorized syllabus? These people don't want anyone to teach the kids to be thinkers who observe and analyze. That was my crime. I taught the kids Herbert Chimhundu's *Chakwesha* and the headmaster told me that I was straying from the accepted path. What path, whose path, and a path for what? Anyway, who told him that I was teaching the kids wrong thinking? Do you know critical analysis and independent thinking, Bunny? I gave those kids a gift. Such a gift that those I taught still remember me. I taught them to be practical and critical. I told them the truth about events that happened during the war, things that my comrades are lying about today. I taught my kids to get to the root of ideas, the root of creativity. My kids knew more than their teachers because I had empowered them to think. That is what they fired me for. If ever I went mad it was after I had left teaching, but I'm not mad. If it was that they thought my mind was too advanced for the kids I was teaching and that I should teach at the university, I might agree. Right now they see me as trash, like an ownerless bin by the roadside. But that is a lie; there is nothing without an owner. Never. When you see me as I am, I am not what you think. Do you know?"

"Yeah, you're right, old man," I replied, trying to see where he was taking this.

"Don't think I'm talking so much because I am drunk. I am telling you that they are mistaken about me. I am not crazy at all. I am not. I refuse. It's not possible. I said I'm not! I am not a house left in a ghost town or the gun that I buried under a huge baobab in Dande. I am not donkey shit in an abandoned field. No, I am not. I am not a child's shoe hanging displayed at a station or a madman's clothing that no one touches at the market. I'm not at all. I am a full snuffbox. I am a path with travelers. A nest full of wasps, a honeycomb with larvae. Do you know, young man Bunny, where I come from there are also people. I get onto a bus and actually pay my fare. When I get home, my Ma, that old lady you saw, says, 'Hello, he's here, catch and slaughter a cockerel for him.' So what makes these people view me as a hobo? It was not a mistake to have fought in the war. It was not. I fought so that we all could be haves, all eat, and all prosper, so that if we starve, we all starve, not for only one man to have excess."

He lifted the bottle to his mouth and took a long draft. I did not want to say anything. He was overburdening me with things to think about when my own thoughts were tired from seeking out answers to life's questions. I was waiting for him to go on. What could I say?

"They are madmen, those people are mad! We are all crazy, lunatics all. Dogs, swine, human scum. Bulbuls, shameless bulbuls that lie to other birds that they kill snakes, when it is merely the sloughed skin. Then, when they see a real snake, they say that they are coming from church where the deacon has forbidden them to kill snakes. They are bulbuls. You know the habits of these bulbuls are very bad. They shut up other birds at the fig tree and leap all over the tree selecting ripe fruit. You hear it say,

'Izvi ndezvangu, Izvi ndezvangu. Izvi ndezvemukoma wangu ari kurwara. Izvi ndezvangu. Izvi ndezvangu. Izvi ndezvemuzukuru wangu ari kumba.'

'This is mine, this is mine. This is for my older brother who is sick. This is mine. This is mine. This is for my nephew at home.'

As if it were capable of eating all the fruit on that tree. Crazy. Really crazy!"

He was standing up and shouting now. I was worried about the embarrassment if Magi, who had promised to come today, should arrive in the midst of all this.

"So I don't see myself staying here. I want to go kumusha and stay there with my old mother and father. Harare has nothing to give me and I don't understand it. It is full of crazy people who regard others as being madder than them. Madmen! You know, my young brother Bunny, when you swallow a pip it's not that you have confidence in your throat but in the other end where it must eventually emerge. I may not go to church but I know

God exists and you guys are punching God with your fists here in Harare."

I was shocked. Was Hamundigone not referring to my dreams where I dreamed I was hitting God with my fists. I felt hot and sweaty.

"Well, let me tell you something, young brother, when you hit God like that, when he hits back it will be a sucker punch that will leave your mind blistered and your lungs punctured."

He became silent as though searching for something to say. I was now scared. I was scared of my dreams.

"Bunny, do you know that if you steal you'll be arrested? So, let some things well alone, like a sister's breast. Know that a child is not punished for stealing peanuts, but to teach him that peanuts are not to be stolen. What I am saying is self-evident. Do you hear?"

He looked at me with red, red eyes. I nodded, pulling off the label on my bottle of Lion Lager. I was no longer with him.

"Bunny, Harare is full of madmen. Where have you ever seen a dog being turned into a wife? Or that a man becomes another man's husband? It's amazing, Bunny. It's rather like hearing that a banana now has pips. So then if that's how it is, where are we going, for what and with whom, and when we get there, what shall we do when we are all crazy?" He looked at me as though in need of an answer, but I did not know how to reply.

"I'm leaving Harare to you who are keen on it. If you say I'm mad I don't care. You sane ones remain here while we the mad go kumusha. But you are also mad. You will stay and look after Charity. I want you to be my eyes here, because I won't have these kids grow up to be dogs and lunatics. Charity is old enough so that I no longer consider her a kid but there's Reuben. Watch over him. If he were not starting school this year I would take him with me but the school at kumusha is too far away. If there's any problem, Shamva is not far from Harare; you saw it when we went to bury Maud, and you can come and tell me. I will only come at month ends."

"Have you spoken to Charity and the maid?" I enquired, surprised that he was really going.

"I'm done with them already. They know that I am going today. Mai Jazz is useless, she's a fool, and that's why I did not ask her to be responsible here. She just might allow my sister Charity to stay with her boyfriend like my niece Heaven."

"If you are going today I could drop you off in Bindura as I'm taking my sister to the school she will be teaching at in Mount Darwin."

"Why not, my man? But I want to go via Mai Jazz's and fetch Harare."

I did not understand which Harare he was now talking about.

"I told Mai Jazz that he is a very good dog if only he is well cared for, so Harare is going to be my friend kumusha. The dog asks no questions, does not think I am mad, so we will get on. Mai Jazz wanted to deny me the dog. I asked her just one question. If she had answered it, I would have left Harare with her," he stated, uncapping another beer bottle.

"What did you say to her?" I asked, just so that I had something to say.

"I asked her what she wanted Harare for. And she failed to answer."

He wiped sweat off his forehead.

"Some people will die like dogs. That dog is too old; it is Zimbabwe's age because it was born the year we got independence. So why does she want it? The time is well past when it was of any use. Now it can't even catch a lame hare. Most likely it would run from the hare. It's now a dog in name only because you can even hear from its barking that it has teeth missing. She should find a new one if she's keen on dogs rather than insisting on that old one. Let it come home with me where it can lie in the shade. But see what madness does. Imagine being left a dog as the legacy of your fleeing white bosses. Is it any wonder the dogs steal? They used to have plenty but now they no longer have . . ."

He did not say any more. He was staring at the gate. I did not notice when Magi arrived. They looked at each other like people who knew each other well and had things they wanted to say to each other. But where would Magi know this old man from? I thought I was either drunk or mad.

Charity

Bunny brought Uncle Hamundigone from kumusha yesterday. Judging from his conversations these days, I think he's now totally crazy. But, surprisingly, Bunny says that he's OK and we seem crazier than Uncle. Can you believe it? Yesterday, Reuben ended up wetting himself in fear of Uncle. One good thing about him is that his madness is only verbal. He does not show any violence apart from toward Heaven, whom he wanted to kill over the issue of her making Reuben do things that even now are hard to talk about. How could she make a baby like Reuben do such disgusting things? I don't know what would have happened if Reuben had been unable to talk.

"Aunty, my thing is sore." Reuben came to me with the fly of his shorts open.

"What? It's too bad. I told you that if you don't wear underpants the zip will nip you. Pull your shorts down, let's see."

What I saw left me weak. If his mother were still with us, this is one thing that would have ended any relationship between her and Mai Heaven and her daughter. OK, Heaven is not much of a person. She does whatever enters her head. She is too spoiled, but I never thought she would take advantage of the time we left Reuben with her when we went kumusha for just three days. I don't know what her problem was to commit such an act of child abuse, given that she has that little shameless man of hers who stays at his mother-in-law's.

With his shorts pulled down, I saw that Reuben's penis was covered with pimples and sores. As soon as I touched him he screamed. I didn't know what to do. I told Uncle Hamundigone since he was the only adult at hand. Bunny had gone to work. Uncle examined Reuben and said he should go to the doctor.

"It's so sore. Heaven played with my thing and put it in hers. I cried, but she would not let me go and she said that if I told anyone she would take me to the kombi people who would chop off my head."

We did not say much going to and coming from the doctor. Uncle suggested that we pass by Mai Heaven's house. If Heaven hadn't managed to get away and lock herself in the toilet, she certainly would have been killed by Uncle because he slapped her so hard her face went grey. She grumbled from inside the toilet, but we could tell she was guilty. If it wasn't for my mother, who had to come from kumusha to help sort things out, Heaven would have been slaughtered by Uncle. He nearly had her arrested.

We were all relieved when Reuben healed fast after treatment and the blood tests the doctor took showed that he did not have the dreaded infection. But still it is sickening. Such a young kid and your aunt's kid at that.

My mother wanted to take Reuben with her, but Bunny suggested that it would be better for him to stay with me, since he was due to start school in a few months and it would be difficult for him to school kumusha seeing how the school was so far away.

Uncle Hamundigone was given this house, our sister's, in which he can raise Reuben. But I don't know if I will ever get used to him. He says that he is here to look after Reuben, me, and the house. Bunny said that he wanted to bring his dog Harare, but my father said to leave it. He says that Harare is what will draw him back kumusha, not the people. Uncle behaves as if he were not my brother. I know that it is his long absence from home when he was at war that makes it seem as if we were not siblings. Now he seems like a stranger because of the way he behaves. I'm scared that one day he will want to come to my college and will embarrass me. Bunny now feels more like a relative to me.

Yesterday, Uncle Hamundigone was too much and embarrassed me when we were going to Sister Mai Heaven's in Unit D. He scared me. We were waiting for kombis to Makoni via Zengeza. We were at the Chitungwiza council head office. It was so hot that Reuben and I sheltered under an umbrella. Uncle was just pacing about in that hot sun. A crowd of Mapostori arrived. I think they were going to attend a church service somewhere. They were the ones with flowing beards and rods and a bevy of women with babies on their backs.

As soon as the Mapostori arrived Uncle burst into laughter. The Mapostori simply looked at him and ignored him. Uncle laughed like a small kid being tickled then abruptly became silent. The sudden silence shocked me. He strode to the Mapostori and came to a halt before them. He was acting like a choirmaster in front of his choir. Passersby were stopping to watch Uncle's antics. As for me, you can't imagine the embarrassment. I gripped Reuben, who was scared of Uncle. I was afraid that people would know that we were together.

He coughed and looked at the people, his eyes watering from the laughter and the coughing. His face glistened with perspiration. He said, "I'm quiet now, I won't laugh anymore."

The people continued to look at him.

"Mapostori, you are blessed and you are exalted because you pray, you attend church services, and you fast. God be with you. I have already sinned against Him so much that I no longer want to nauseate Him by continually going before Him to repent, for I know I will sin again," Uncle said, looking at the Mapostori.

"What do you say, you of the white garments? Are your hearts as clean as your garments? Are you committed and resolute? Answer me, Mapostori."

No one answered. They were seeing a madman as far as I was concerned.

"Why do you not answer me, madzibaba and madzimai? Is it because your hearts are weighed down by troubles, or perhaps you see me as a madman?"

No one answered. Two full kombis passed.

Uncle resumed. Now he was really acting crazy. "Hear me, you who are listening, because I, who cannot see, saw the things that happen in our lives."

"Amen," said two young men who were each holding a beer bottle.

"Amen! Now say hallelujah!"

"Hallelujah!" the beer boys said.

"Hear me now, you commuters, drinkers, madzibaba and madzimai."

"Amen!" The beer guys yelled again.

"We go to the fields but have we ever seen the harvest? Now we are starving as if we never tilled the land. We agreed to work together, but we did not listen to the advice of the agricultural specialist."

"Hallelujah!"

"So we asked what kind of farmers are these, who do their work by letter only. Imagine phoning your future in-laws instead of sending a munyai and demanding to know how much the bride price will be."

"That's modernity, old man," one of the drunken young men said.

Uncle did not answer but went on with his sermon in the scorching sun.

"That's why we once told you that Magaisa fleeced us for real. He made us plough with hungry oxen, and cultivate the crops with broken hoes. The little maize we got he demanded even though he knew we would starve, and we gave it to him as he was the chief."

"Old man, carry on with your story," said one of the drunken boys. They were the only ones talking to Uncle.

"Give me time. Meat does not immediately brown upon being put in the pot," replied Uncle.

A kombi came. I considered going and leaving him there but dreaded the thought that he might embarrass me more. You can never be too sure of Uncle. I don't understand him.

Some of the Mapostori got on the kombi and only a few people were left at the bus stop. I thought Uncle would stop what he was doing but the two drunken boys kept urging him on.

"Keep up the gospel, old man."

"After the harvest, Magaisa snatched all we had toiled for. We realized that this was daylight sorcery but no one dared complain. The little money that he gave us would not even cover bus fare. Why would we need to go on the bus anyway? Those who were coming from the place we wanted to go told us that neither bread nor sugar were available there either, so we were just existing by the grace of God. That is why I say you Mapostori are blessed."

"Amen," came from one of the elders among the Mapostori, whose shaven head shone like a mirror.

"I saw that we would have to survive by grazing on grass, provided the grass had not already been sold. If we failed to survive on the grass from the rain God sent, we would have to eat the grass thatching our huts, leaving our roofs wide open to the skies. We will see God on his throne and he will take pity on us because, apart from his mercy, no one else will feel for us."

He paused in his speech, then wiped the perspiration from his brow. An empty kombi arrived but no one would get on, as they all wanted to hear Uncle speaking. Madness can be perplexing. I was tired of standing. It was hot. The kombi crew was annoyed because no one wanted to get on and one shouted, "If you listen to the thoughts of a madman you too become madmen." It was the hwindi who shouted this as he hung on to the vehicle's door.

"But people, why has God failed to take pity on us? Is it that he is wrathful over the way we, his creatures, spend our days? Is it because someone has decided to rewrite the Bible in his own way, what God had already written? For what? Would that make you into God? No. Feel sorry for that person. He has energy for that because he is well fed. He does not even know what part of the body hurts when one is hungry. Oh, so that is how you guys behave? Hear the way my stomach rumbles. The rumbling of many days' hunger. We fart freely, even in front of children."

Uncle's voice echoed as though it were coming from the mountains, as if it were rusty, as if it were hollow.

"She laughed to herself one day, a crone without a single tooth, and her mouth like a cave. The crone was gray from lack of fat to feed her and anoint her skin. It surprised people to hear someone laughing when everyone else was dizzy with hunger. They looked at the crone who no longer had cheeks, only jaws. That crone laughed and then fell down. That is how she died. She died with hunger written all over her face like the lies that lovers write to each other in their letters. But that is not all. A babe cried, it cried with a rotten voice, a weak voice, a voice stinking with suffering. It had suckled its mother's dehydrated teats and cried because out of those breasts did not come milk, but death—rank and ghastly.

"Even I got a shock when I took off my overalls. I thought myself healthy but was stunned to see bones emerging from the overalls. As the siren went, I wondered what I would do for lunch apart from whiling away the time and hunger by playing checkers. We had worked so hard that our hands were swollen and we could not even wipe our lips, which were white as though powdered with flour.

"When I was going home to a house that does not belong to me, where I live in a backyard shack, I saw buses carrying bodies whose occupants were no longer present. It was in Rezende Street. Their bodies no longer had hearts. When I glanced at the shop across the road, I noticed their missing hearts packed on a shelf, for sale. Their owners had sold them to get bus fare. What would they do the following day?

"As I stood in the bus queue I saw a young man holding a bible and preaching about Matthew 24, saying that people should repent, as the Kingdom of Heaven is approaching, but no one gave him an ear. That is what scares me about being a preacher, that I might become a destroyer instead of a preacher. In the course of preaching I might tell people things that God would not approve of and maybe make them give me money so that I could drive around in a flashy car.

"Forgive them and have mercy on them that sin against us. But why, you Mapostori, why do they sin against us day after day? Give us this day our daily bread, but where will we get it when it goes up in price day after day? Yesterday sugar, today bread, tomorrow cooking oil . . .

"They have failed to keep God's name sacred and they've even forgotten that He exists. Even His Kingdom, which we wish to come, will not, because the church and political leaders want kingship for themselves. They no longer know that it is God's will that keeps us alive, for they feel that they hold all time in their hands.

"Do not deliver them from their evil because they do not forgive us our slightest sins. In temptation is where they want to stay. In addition, everything we give to God, the power and the glory, they also want. But what is it? What is it really?"

"Amen. Amen. Amen." The audience acted as if possessed. They shouted till I was submerged in their voices. It confused me that I am no believer and I think of Uncle as a madman. It put fear in me.

Reuben

I am scared of Uncle, but sometimes he makes me laugh. Aunt Charity and Uncle Bunny lie to me that Mummy went to South Africa. Yesterday Uncle Hamundigone told me that Mummy died. So if she died, has she melted like ice cream, like Tonderai and Joe said? They said that when people die they are buried and then they melt like ice cream and never come back. That's why I refused an ice cream yesterday when Uncle Bunny offered to buy me one.

Uncle Hamundigone said that if I carry on refusing to eat he will sell me to the kombis. I am scared of the kombi guys because Mummy said that if I get on a kombi alone they would chop my head off.

Even Aunty Rutendo at crèche told us not to get on kombis alone. She also said if we do, we would have our heads chopped off. They say when your head is chopped off it gets sold to a butchery in South Africa. I once asked Mummy if she sees the people's heads in butcheries when she goes to South Africa but she scolded me.

Uncle Bunny told me these were all lies because his brother's friend is a kombi driver. But I did not want to get on a kombi when they said we should go to Makoni.

And I don't like going to Aunt Mai Heaven's. Their home is dirty. Their sofas are torn. And they smell of wee wee. Sister Heaven is greedy. She grabbed my meat pie from me, which I was eating when we arrived. She laughs like Tonderai's dog that steals. I hate her. She looks like the witch I saw in a picture book at Joe's house.

"Reuben, you are going to be stingy like your mother!" Heaven said. Mummy said I must like her, but I don't want to because she acts like a mad person. She says that Uncle Hamundigone is mad, but it is she who is mad. She swears, and I know Aunty Rutendo at crèche has forbidden us to swear.

Today we are at Heaven's. I came with Aunty Charity and Uncle. If she says that she wants me to stay behind with her, I will refuse. She plays with my thing for peeing and leaves it sore, then she laughs. If she does it again I'm going to tell my Uncle Bunny. If I tell Aunty Charity she won't do anything because Heaven is not afraid of her. I don't like Heaven because she's mean. She has a stinky friend. Uncle Hamundigone shouted at him and Heaven did not like it. Heaven nearly fought with Uncle Hamundigone.

"Who is this person sitting in my sister's home as though it's his?" Uncle shouts as he enters the house. We were taught not to make noise when we speak at crèche. Aunty Charity's hand holding mine is sweating. The skin cream she is using is not hers but my mother's. I told her at home that it was my mother's cream and she shouted at me. She said if I talked too much she would take me to the kombis. I am scared of the kombis.

It's my mother's cream smelling so nice on her hands. Aunt Mai Heaven is not here today. I don't know any of the people in her house. They are all drinking. I'm cold.

"Hey, why don't you answer? What's it with the beer so early in the morning?" Uncle never greets people when he arrives, he simply says what he likes. Mummy once told me that a person who does not greet people has bad manners. Heaven comes out from one of the rooms. She has on purple tights and a body top that looks like my mother's.

"You stole my Mummy's body top!"

Aunt Charity pinches me to shut me up. She does it painfully.

Heaven looks at me and frowns. Then she says, "This one will be evil like his mother!"

"Heaven, leave the kid alone. Why do you act like a witch?" Uncle likes to talk about scary things like witches.

"Uncle, your sister is not here. When she is not here, you have to behave like a normal human being."

"Heaven, if you think that just because you talk crap to your mother you can do the same to me, I will blast that face till it's the same color as your lipstick."

"Uncle, you can beat your own child, not me. If you dare hit me, I will set some gangsters on you and you will have new scars to add to the bullet scars you already have." Heaven is fearless. She glares with her red eyes as she talks.

"Let me just sit myself down. Mad people should be ignored. Come here Reuben, my nephew." I don't want to sit near Uncle Hamundigone. He stinks. But Mummy told me that I should not say people smell. Adults are very strange. Mummy is the one who told me I should tell the truth.

I fell asleep leaning on Uncle Hamundigone who was talking on and on. He was laughing and talking loudly. I only woke up when we were back home.

Bunny

As we were drinking beer, as usual, Uncle Hamundigone said:

> "Does not each and every one do what they please?
> So I want to sleep until all sleep is gone,
> I want to sleep until I wake, rather than be woken up.
> I want to eat till I throw up on the plate,
> I want to lie till you all say I speak the truth.

Is that not freedom?
I want to not wash till I smell good.
I want to not listen till you no longer talk to me,
But what I most want to do,
I want to rule until there is no one left to rule.
I want to remain alone with my walking stick,
So that if it were possible,
I would like to buy God, so I can live forever.
Why not when we are in Africa!"

He laughed a carefree laugh, of one who has few things to give him sleepless nights or make him dream thorny dreams like me. If only I had freedom in my heart like Uncle Hamundigone. He has said, hasn't he, that he no longer seeks much. This is one person who understands life in Zimbabwe.

Voices of the Mad

Uncle Hamundigone was pleased to see Bunny's sister, Magi. Funny how things go. Life is like a feather blown by the wind, you don't know where it will land once the wind has lifted it. They've met again, these two who have a child together. But Magi seems uncertain about Uncle's behavior. Uncle has already begun courting her anew. He is funny. He said to Magi, "You are the one who gave me wings. I flew and my heart was full."

Magi

I am really scared now. Today Bunny fell asleep before me. I reminisced about things that used to happen when I was at college. I cannot believe it. The past now seems like a dream.

When I met up with Hamundigone, the father of my child, I was very pleased, but I'm also concerned if he is still the same man that I once knew. He has somehow become disturbed, yet I still feel for him deep down.

What does one do when this happens? I don't know. This is all because Bunny is unwell. He is not so sick that he can't eat or has to lie down, but he is sick in such a way that only our parents can intervene. It looks like a chivanhu problem. The problem for some of us is that chivanhu is now leagues and leagues away from us. I have to think hard to remember what the color of snuff is. Anyway, that's life, right?

Now I am undergoing this punishment where I have to be up all night watching over Bunny and making sure he does not wake up and run off or do something dangerous. He's been asleep for quite some time now. He says he needs alcohol so he won't dream that he's growing feathers in his mouth. This is really scary. Yesterday I was reading a book, sitting on a chair, and I felt my strength drain away. Bunny turned over and looked as if he were struggling with something. He got up and sat on the floor, shaking his head and sweating. He then started shouting,

"I told them a long time ago
That I don't eat horse meat,
Pork, or puppy meat,
But they keep dishing it up for me.
Dishing up huge pieces!"

I just gaped at him. If it were not the school holidays, I would not be here, I would have an excuse. I thought to wake him up because I saw that he was asleep. I put down the book I was reading then crept toward him to shake him, even though I was scared. I knelt by his side and noticed that he was sweating and breathing heavily. He stank of the whisky he had drunk with Hamundigone earlier in the afternoon. I took hold of his shoulder to wake him to ask him who it was giving him this meat. I felt sorry for him and feared him at the same time. I thought that the situation needed our parents, not me. I am a mere child, totally unqualified for this.

"Bunny," I said in a voice that was not my own. Whatever I wanted to say next fled.

He started and shoved me so that I nearly hit the floor with the back of my head.

"Eh! Who are you? I told you already that my mind is tired. Why are you doing this to me?"

"I'm Magi, your sister."

"Is it really Magi?" he asked, as if he had met someone he knew in an inappropriate place.

"Yes, it's me," I answered, afraid of the raspiness in my voice.

"When did I come here, Magi?"

"From where, Brother?"

"Yes, Magi. That's what I am asking, from where did I come? Talk, Magi. I said, where did I come from?"

I almost wet myself. I have never been as stumped as I was then. Even the air I was breathing began to feel like tear gas.

He resumed talking. "I came. I returned. You are surprised. Actually it's my fault. I came from an unexpected direction, at a time you did not expect. That is exactly what Jesus will do to you when he returns. He will return when you are engaged in gossip. What will you say? Anyway, welcome me. Don't you know me anymore? Don't be like that. When did you forget me? If you have forgotten me, I will only tell you who I am after you give me mahewu. No, I don't want the mahewu you give to schoolchildren that has not been fermented for long enough. I want the one which smells of alcohol."

I didn't know what to say. I was confused and felt tears coming. We don't have a history of mental disturbance in my family. Where was this coming from?

Suddenly he sighed and touched my hand. He was now the Bunny that I know.

"Magi, why are you wiping my face?"

"You are sweating, Brother."

"Why don't you go to bed?"

"I'll go just now. I just wanted to make sure you sleep well."

"I'm not sick, Magi, I'm quite well," he said, feeling his face. His eyes were red like peri-peri.

We sighed together. Bunny laughed and said, "Did you see Uncle Hamundigone?"

"Yes, I saw him. I was glad to see him after such a long time."

"Let's hope you can discuss your relationship and see if you can bring up Rudo together."

"I don't know, we'll see."

It is still troubling me, what decision to make. Let me just wait and see what happens. Perhaps we will get married and I'll be able to live with my kid. Remaining single is more suitable for people like Kundai who is committed to a life of prostitution in the Avenues. I wonder why she's thrown herself away like that. She says that she doesn't do it all the time, only part-time to supplement her income when she is short. So she has not abandoned her college habit of going out with men for money. It's tough.

I realized when we were still at college that Kundai had a hidden corner in her life. One thing she was good at was concealing it. One would never have thought that's how she was. One thing she could talk about without hiding it was that she was a munozi.

"Magi, I am not oblivious to the changes that are taking place in our lives locally as well as globally. My friend, everything is changing. The cars that were driven in the fifties are not the ones being driven today. Even the way we dress is modern; it's becoming more outrageous. In short, life is changing. If anyone is unhappy because we speak and dress as we wish then they must leave Zimbabwe because this country belongs to us all, the decent people and us mad ones. Did Zhakata not sing, 'Because the nation is you and me and our environment.'"

"Do you suppose there are people who would hate someone for their way of speaking?" I asked, to see what she thought.

"Magi, do you remember telling me about your kid's father and how he was a teacher? I'm sure I shared a ride with him on a commuter omnibus and he annoyed me. You said he was a teacher at Mavhuradona where you went to school, didn't you, and that he is a war vet? I am sure it was him. I disliked him because he insulted me for my way of life. Because I am a munozi. I wanted to tell you that day but you were under a lot of stress because of the matter with that other old man of yours.

"Magi, people need to know that our way of life, our culture, certainly has changed since the days of Nehanda and Chaminuka."

"But Kundai, it might have changed, but does it need mending? And does it necessarily have to be a totally new culture that comes in new packages so that those who played a part in its making are left behind after having failed to comprehend it?"

"Magi, I have to tell you. I know that there is all that stuff about no longer respecting our elders and so forth, but is a person born to fear other people? Are you born to live a life that people want you to live? That is what is called oppression. Each person should do what is good for him and what he feels makes him free when doing it. As for me—smoke, cow dung, totems, drinking gourds, wells, and grass thatched huts, I leave to you."

Kundai could not be silenced when it came to these issues. What I liked about her was that she could look at issues clearly.

Life is fascinating. Life is rough. When we run away from the so-called primitive life, the sophisticated life is confusing and extreme. Even when you think you are on top of it, it can surprise and leave you floored. I think we want too much as people so that we become fools of materialism. We make ourselves out to be very special creatures, educated and too smart to kneel down and blow a fire on the hearth. We make for ourselves all sorts of conveniences, some of which border on vanity. We want our toilet paper to be the softest and when we are done with the business we look for air fresheners to dispel any lingering odors. Isn't shit supposed to smell like shit? Then we look for scented soap to wash our hands, towels to dry them on, and a mirror in which to examine ourselves, even though we know who we are.

Kundai says she started flashing her body as a sex worker in the Avenues from the time we were in college. She said, "I did it occasionally to supplement payout when things were not balancing up." Even the job that she was given at Bunny's work place was a transaction. How will it all end? The proverb says, "You can only swim once in a pool infested with crocodiles; the second time you will find them awake."

I had to let Kundai know my concerns. “But why do you cheapen yourself like that? Aren’t you scared of AIDS?”

“My friend, tell me which way is not death? I cheated on my husband and was divorced, kicked out like a dog, and I left my two children behind. Ever since we parted a lot has happened. My income is not enough even though I have a degree. How does a degree help when sugar and bread are going up? When you fell pregnant you had your mother to look after your baby, so you had no worries.”

I don’t think I really know who Kundai is. She said she would come here this weekend. She was fired from Bunny’s workplace for incompetence. She claims to be doing consultancy work, but what exactly she won’t say. I am now uncomfortable about telling people that I know her. I don’t. It is like this with most people in Harare; they are like phantoms.

“What are you thinking about, Magi? Why are you quiet?” I had forgotten that I was with Bunny in his room.

“Sorry. I am trying to process many things. Let me go so you can sleep.” I thought maybe I had overstayed my welcome from the time Bunny had woken up complaining about the huge pieces of meat.

“No, Magi. Stay.” Bunny made me so uncomfortable when he pleaded with me to stay while holding my hand.

“Magi, life is difficult, my friend.” He paused for a while, giving me time to get over the fact that he had called me his friend. I remained silent. But I could hear my heart beating right in my ear.

“Magi, nothing will remain as it is. That’s the way it goes. There’s nothing new that will surprise you. That’s the world. We’ve seen it all, heard it all, and spoken about it all when we still had humanity. We have joined the rats in their race and we are way ahead. We should learn to give time a chance. I am now afraid of life, Magi. I don’t know if there’s anything left for me. I am scared and I don’t know how to tell you. But I am scared. I’m scared that perhaps I might be, well, I might be ill. I’m scared of the dreaded disease. I wanted to go for tests, but I’m unable to, because I’m so scared.”

He was silent for a bit. Now I could feel my heart beating in my mouth. I said nothing. I kept quiet because there was nothing to say.

A baby started crying outside. I'm sure it's the baby next door to Maud's. They have a baby that cries almost to death. The way it cries is frightening.

Bunny sighed. "My problem now is how long I can continue being scared. I am suffering because of this life of fear. I don't know whether I am infected, but I am scared because I was Maud's lover and I am sure that she died from the disease. That's my problem."

I've never been as at a loss for words my whole life as I was at that moment. I pretended to clear my throat and kept silent.

"Is there any hope for tomorrow, Magi?"

I felt as if I had been pricked by a needle in a tender spot. I heard myself speak like a sage. "Brother, this life is ours, but it is not ours. But I want you to know that,

You are not a house left in a ghost town
You are not donkey shit in an abandoned field
Or a child's lost shoe hanging in a bus
You are none of those.

You are a path with travelers on it
A nest full of wasps in it
A honeycomb with larvae in it.

Where you come from there are people.
You get onto a bus
When you arrive we say,
'Hello, he's here. Catch a cockerel for him.'

So don't be afraid
You are not a vagabond.

If there are problems, we see them out together as one people. I'm with you, my brother. You can count on me."

I don't remember the other stuff that I said. I don't know anymore if it had any meaning. As for me, I started to fear life as well, for it had never occurred to me that one might be walking around, doing normal everyday things, and yet be carrying HIV.

Mai Tanya in Spirit

I realized and understood, when there was no time left, that living a life of fearing others, fearing the opinions of others, is our greatest undoing and my biggest regret. We are all born free, but there are those who have their freedom snatched away, and others who willingly give their freedom away. And there are those who find themselves oppressed from the beginning. Yet freeing yourself requires no money, only standing up for yourself and telling yourself that you are as human as the next person. Trying to please others by doing what does not please us is what destroys us. Failure to say that this won't do. We are afraid to be called cowards, sellouts, or to be rejected. Why do we fear to be alone when we were born alone? A person is human because each of us has their own life. Maybe it changes when one weds and "your people become my people."

But letting yourself be exploited by your partner's people to please him is no life. A person ought to be free to do what they feel is right for them. I am not saying people should adopt Western ideas that kinship is burdensome. No. It is relatives that make our lives worth living. But having relatives that snatch your freedom away for their pleasure, or so that you might be an outcast, is the same as being alone. The greater part of the time we spend trying to please others does not help because generally they don't care about us. Selfishness.

However, a person who really cares for you and loves you does not snatch away your freedom. He does not treat you as though you owe him something every time you meet. With some people it is better not to see them because every time you meet they will be dying to pluck feathers from your wings because you are independent.

The elders were correct when they said the tooth is a fool; it shows itself when one smiles even for people they don't like.

But I say it is not the tooth that is the fool. The fools are you and me who fail to tell the truth; the truth might be that I like you because you have money or a good job. It's about parasitism and forming friendships or relationships that can benefit you financially. I would not befriend a dip tank supervisor if I had no cattle. It is bad for us to think the world owes us something. We only live once. Even if we pretend to love someone when we don't love them wholeheartedly, one day the worm inside the apple will be seen by the holes it makes.

All things need a time of transformation. We are headed for trouble. There is going to come a time when you visit your nephew, your very sister's son, and he will ask you, standing at his threshold, what you want. Because whatever used to bind us when we still had humanity and love for each other as aunt and nephew has passed. The source of the problem is economic hardship. It causes some to try to stick to others and suck off them like fleas.

It's tough, but people should be free. People should be self-reliant. The days of borrowing sugar from my neighbor are over. If someone needs something from another, he should wait to be given it and not seize it. I tried to do my bit. Those I owed I paid back. If I overlooked anyone, I crave forgiveness so that I can travel this otherworldly journey without hindrance.

Saru

Some people are amazing. They think that only they are human and others are not. They believe that they own other people. But then you can only own a person whose thoughts you know. I might smile at you because I respect you, but you might think you own me now. But no, my people. A person is their own person, even when they have only one eye or are struggling in life. I may be poor, and take your orders with a smile, but never think that you own me. I also dream of freedom, of throwing parties and dancing my poverty away. I declare war against poor employers who treat those poorer than them like dogs.

We will meet, inevitably.

Hamundigone

A long time ago I told my sister, the mother of Heaven, that one must choose what they really want in life. You can't be both a women's leader at church and a mobilizer of political party supporters at the same time. That is confusing. I don't get it.

Charity

Death? What exactly does death do? My sister's death has left me devastated. I now have no one to ask this and that. What about the kid? What about her house? Who will Reuben stay with when I want to marry? With Uncle Hamundigone? Will that work? Sister Mai Heaven's place is a nonstarter. She has failed to raise her daughter properly and will not be able to raise Reuben.

There are times when the absence of people, resources, and ideas cause the mind to scatter. I feel confused and sometimes I find myself talking to my sister Maud as if she were still here. Sometimes I even think I hear her taking a shower and singing as she used to do. I feel scattered like dead leaves in the wind.

Now that the kids have all gone to school, the ghetto is silent like a mortuary. I've had enough; I'm tired in body and mind. This may be my sister's house, but it feels strange to me without its owner. It needs her to light it up, to tell us what to do. There are times I think about life and its meaning, but it seems a full stop can be placed before you and life immediately ceases.

Sometimes I think about going to the tuck shop or even the big shops and feel happy to be outdoors, but this breath of fresh air does not last, as the neighborhood women point me out and talk over their hedges, "That's the one whose older sister died from AIDS." Some will say, "That Maud was too bigheaded about her flea markets that she started with money from the husband she poisoned."

People! Words! That's why I stay at home. When you go outside, people's unkind words sear your heart. Anyway, sometimes there is no one for me to go out and see or talk to. Life should not feel like a prison like this.

But I should not stress too much about what tomorrow holds; I'll deal with each day as it comes. If only Bunny would continue staying here. He is very helpful. He is the one who knows that there is pension money that Maud received that should still come so that Reuben and I can live off it, since I am here to look after Reuben. I wonder if there are any others who have relatives but are without relationships like me. Although I try to avoid it, when I feel overburdened and about to crash-land, I can always go to my mother for help. Our kumusha is quite near, but my mother is still mourning Maud and also needs a shoulder to lean on.

Magi

I am sad that I have to go back to my school at Nyakasikana. It is good to be here and to be in touch again. I have seen my friend Cleodia—she had come to see her father Hamundigone. Bunny is not doing too badly. He went for counseling and had tests to see if he is positive but the results are not yet out. I think he is better because he now sleeps alright and has gone back to work.

Hamundigone cried when he saw his daughter Rudo, who had come with my mother from kumusha. She is now a big girl. He said she should come here and stay with her father when she starts school. I hope he will get the job that Bunny told me about, doing industrial training for workers near Harare Hospital. I am interested in Hamundigone, but I want to give myself time to assess before I commit myself.

Bunny is going to be working in Kariba for a week. He said he is taking Charity and Reuben so that they can have a break. I suspect Bunny is in love with Charity, but I told him not to be irresponsible with her. He should wait for the result of his blood test. All he can do is to hope for the best.

Kundai came at the weekend. She looks tired. Even she admitted that she was tired. I did not ask why. As Mtukudzi said, some things should not be asked, and some things should not be stirred up.

She joked with Bunny. That is when I heard that the man who had given her the job at Bunny's workplace had also been fired. Kundai laughed, saying that the man thought that falling off his high horse was not possible.

Kundai looks sick. I hope it is not AIDS. She and Hamundigone recognized each other from their argument on the kombi from Bindura some time back. They nearly opened up the issue again and exchanged words. I did not know who to restrain or what to say. The thing came to an abrupt end when Mai Heaven arrived weeping, telling us that Heaven had killed her husband. She was moaning that her house would be tormented by a ngozi since the man had died in there and that Heaven would probably be sentenced to death. According to those who went to Unit D, the issue was about the son-in-law making the housemaid pregnant, which, when the matter came to light, brought forth the seeds of murder. What ghastly things happen in the ghetto!

VC

Joyi is crazy. She actually thinks I would marry a whore? She will have to have an abortion. She wants to ruin my business.

A Human

When you find yourself being asked when you will return, don't think it is a sign of popularity. Sometimes people look forward to their freedom in your absence. So, now that I am going, don't bother to ask me any questions because I have no answers for you. Just know that I will be back.

Acknowledgments

Thank you Flora Veit-Wild for loving Mapenzi and initiating the translation into English. If I had a way I would give you honorary citizenship for your immense contribution to Zimbabwean literature.

Brian and Jane, it has been a long journey that we have walked together. Thank you for your sincere friendship, patience, and unassuming nature. Zimbabwe misses you dearly!

About the Author

Ignatius Tirivangani Mabasa is a Zimbabwean storyteller, writer, and translator who mainly creates in his mother language—Shona. His love for storytelling and words was nurtured from a young age through traditional oral narratives and folk tales. Mabasa's writing often explores themes of identity, culture, and social justice, drawing from his experiences as a black Zimbabwean living under colonial rule and later during the country's transition to independence. In addition to his writing, Mabasa has taught creative writing in the United States and Canada. His Shona novel *Mapenzi* was mentioned as one of "the most significant books to have come out of Africa," in *The Times Literary Supplement* of August 17, 2001. He is a former Fulbright scholar (USA) and former writer and storyteller in residence (University of Manitoba, Canada). For the past fifteen years he has been giving fresh impetus to Shona folktales by making them available in film form and on social media platforms. Mabasa currently resides in Harare, Zimbabwe. He is a research associate with the School of Languages, Rhodes University, South Africa, and a senior fellow in the Department of Anthropology at the University of Amsterdam. He is currently lecturing at the University of Zimbabwe.